D0166613

LP COP
Copper, Basil.
Jet-lag.

DATE DUE

JET-LAG

Basil Copper

CHIVERS
THORNDIKE

This Large Print book is published by BBC Audiobooks Ltd, Bath, England and by Thorndike Press®, Waterville, Maine, USA.

Published in 2004 in the U.K. by arrangement with the author.

Published in 2004 in the U.S. by arrangement with Basil Copper.

U.K. Hardcover   ISBN 1–4056–3061–2 (Chivers Large Print)
U.K. Softcover   ISBN 1–4056–3062–0 (Camden Large Print)
U.S. Softcover   ISBN 0–7862–6843–3 (Nightingale)

The text of this Large Print edition is unabridged.
Other aspects of the book may vary from the original edition.

Set in 16 pt. New Times Roman.

Printed in Great Britain on acid-free paper.

British Library Cataloguing in Publication Data available

Library of Congress Control Number: 2004107495

CHAPTER ONE

1

'There's a girl to see you,' Stella said breezily. 'She seems to be in some kind of trouble.'

I shifted in my swivel-chair and squinted up toward the cracks in the ceiling.

'That makes two of us,' I said.

Stella's eyes were very clear and very blue as she stared down at me.

'I think it's serious, Mike. She's out in the waiting room.'

I straightened up in the chair and gave Stella one of my best smiles. It was too hot for comfort this morning and I'd been on stake-out too long. Maybe this client would have something more interesting for me.

I had a quick look at myself in the telephone mirror. My image stared back at me, dark and sardonic like always.

'Wheel her on in,' I said.

Stella smiled faintly. Today she wore a red silk shirt, tailored blue jeans with a broad leather belt with a gold buckle and highly polished tan shoes that made a heart-stirring clitter as she went to and from the glassed-in alcove where we do the brewing-up. It wasn't time for coffee yet so she hadn't been doing any clittering but I was looking forward to it.

Both the coffee and the clittering, I mean.

I sat back at my old broadtop and frowned at the beams of sunlight that were coming through the slats in the blinds and stencilling dark shadows on the carpet. Below, on the boulevard, a tangle of overheated metal was contributing a nice layer of carbon monoxide on top of the smog. It's one of the things that makes living in the L.A. basin such a pleasure.

'Does the lady have a name?' I said.

Stella raised her eyebrows, the gold bell of her hair shimmering beneath the lamps.

'My,' she told the filing cabinet. 'We are genteel this morning.'

I grinned. It had been a rough month for Faraday Investigations and even my overdraft was beginning to get an overdraft.

'If this is a case it's about as genteel as you'll see me,' I told her. 'So make the most of it.'

Stella gave me one of her mysterious smiles.

'Tina Matthews,' she said. 'With two tees.'

'I'll make a note of it,' I said. 'It may be important.'

Stella's smile still lingered as she went over toward the door leading to the waiting room.

'What's her trouble?' I said.

Stella shrugged.

'She didn't have time to say.'

She went on out and left me staring at the cracks in the ceiling. I didn't have long to wait. She came back with a tall, fair-haired girl who had niceness written all over her. She was well-proportioned and the lightweight grey suit she wore seemed to accentuate the sensuality behind the demure exterior. If you know what I mean.

She had very red lips and when she opened her generous mouth in a shy smile she revealed a set of white teeth that owed little to Californian dental surgeons. Even without the heavy rimmed tortoise-shell glasses she looked as attractive as a morning in spring looks to the colour section photographers.

She came forward a little, looking at me uncertainly and blinking behind her glasses.

'Mr Faraday?'

I was about to give her my standard reply about that being what it said on the door when I intercepted Stella's smile and changed my sentence. I'm pretty good at the instant sub-editing.

'Take a chair,' I said.

Stella pulled it forward with an adroit movement and the girl sank back gratefully, giving Stella an appreciative glance over her shoulder. She seemed as well-bred as the fashion editor of a New York society magazine. Though one couldn't rely on that too much.

Stella gave me a dry look like she knew what I was thinking and went briskly over toward the alcove.

'We'd all like coffee, I take it,' she said brightly. The Matthews number flushed like it was a sensational idea or something.

'That would be very nice. If you're sure it's no trouble.'

'It's no trouble,' I said. 'I understand you have a problem.'

The girl bit her lip, the expression of her eyes hidden by the light reflecting from her glasses.

'I don't know whether I've done right to come here, Mr Faraday. I've never engaged the services of a private detective before. I may not even be able to afford your fees.'

'There's always a first time, Miss Matthews,' I said. 'And Faraday Investigations is noted for its economical rates.'

'Sometimes we don't get paid at all,' Stella said.

She was back from the alcove, standing in the middle of the room, her arms folded across her breasts. She looked great like that. Her eyes met mine. I stared at the Matthews number again.

'We aren't even going to charge you for the coffee,' I said.

The girl's face lightened. Then it clouded again.

'I hardly know where to begin, Mr Faraday.'

'That's what they all say,' I told her. 'You'll feel better when you've had a cup of coffee. Then you can tell me all about it.'

4

I shovelled a mite more sugar into my cup and looked from its dancing black surface to Stella's concentrated face as her pencil raced across the paper. The Matthews number seemed more relaxed now and she gave a fleeting smile to Stella as she finished taking down her address and phone number. She lived in an apartment block over on the far side of town and I hoped I wouldn't need to go over there very often because there was a major traffic tangle around that section due to large-scale road works.

'It's really about my sister,' the girl went on. She smiled at me apologetically.

'She's only three years older than me but we couldn't be more different. I'm a librarian, working on the academic side.'

She flashed me another brief smile.

'Erika's a night-club entertainer. We're separate worlds entirely. But I wouldn't want you to get the idea we don't get on. We do pretty well most of the time. We've lived together very happily for the last three years, since our parents died.'

I focused my eyes up on the sun-dazzle at the blinds and waited for Stella's gold pencil to come to a halt.

'I'm sure, Miss Matthews,' I said. 'It's maybe

a little unusual but not unknown for sisters to take diametrically opposed lines of work.'

The girl's tortoise-shell glasses glinted again as she looked from me to Stella. She stared at me helplessly.

'It's just that I'm so out of my depth, Mr Faraday.'

'In what way?'

'Erika's changed a lot in the last six months. I'm afraid she may have been getting into bad company.'

Stella slightly raised her eyebrows.

'That's one of the hazards of night club life, Miss Matthews,' I said. 'They attract a lot of undesirable characters.'

Stella smiled at me over the girl's shoulder.

'Where is this place she works?' I said.

There was a pink flush on Tina Matthews' cheeks now.

'It's a spot called The Blue Parrot. You may have heard of it. She has a contract to sing there twice nightly.'

I nodded.

'I've heard of it all right, Miss Matthews. It's one of the best of its type. Your sister isn't working at the seedy end. She must be pretty good.'

Tina Matthews caught one of the white teeth with her lower lip in a little nervous action.

'Erika's a very good singer, Mr Faraday. She's doing well. But I don't like the friends she's been keeping company with. And then when she didn't turn up lately . . .'

She broke off and sat staring down into her half-empty coffee cup.

'You'll have to explain that,' I said.

The Matthews number gave another of her helpless shrugs. She was pretty good at them and she was giving me a wide selection this morning. The corners of her mouth suddenly dropped so that I thought she was going to burst into tears.

'She's never done anything like this before, Mr Faraday. I'm worried sick and at my wits' end.'

'If you'd just explain I'd have some idea of your problem,' I told her.

'I'm sorry, Mr Faraday. I said I was no good at explanations. Erika didn't come home the other night. She works pretty late, of course. She's never in before three a.m. because her last spot is at one o'clock and it's a fair drive home after she gets changed and out of make-up. But she's never stayed out at night before.'

I sat up a little straighter in my swivel chair.

'When was this?' I said.

'Three nights ago, Mr Faraday. Erika's a very nice girl. She never stayed out all night in her life before to my knowledge. I'm afraid something may have happened to her.'

I stared at her for a long moment.

'You mean to say she's been missing for three days and you've had no message?'

7

Tina Matthews nodded.

'Have you contacted The Green Parrot?' I said. Stella gave me a pained look over the girl's shoulder.

'The Blue Parrot, Mr Faraday,' the Matthews number corrected me. 'Yes, of course. I rang them straight away. I've been ringing them every day since. I can't get hold of the management but the message I keep getting from the staff is that she's gone away and they don't know when she'll be back.'

I picked up my coffee and got some more of it down me.

'And you haven't reported this to the police?'

The girl's eyes were wide beneath the heavy-rimmed glasses.

'I didn't think it necessary, Mr Faraday. I kept thinking Erika would ring with some explanation.'

Stella put down her pencil and rose to get some re-fills. The girl drained her cup and relinquished it to Stella with a grateful expression.

'And you haven't been over to The Blue Parrot?' I said.

Tina Matthews shook her head.

'I'm much too shy, Mr Faraday,' she said simply. 'I've never been inside one of those places. I wouldn't know how to go about such enquiries. And what would be the point, anyway. They've already said she's gone away.'

Stella came back and quietly put the re-filled cups in front of us. I waited until she'd re-seated herself before I went on.

'So you want me to ask some discreet questions,' I said.

'That's right, Mr Faraday. I'd be most grateful.'

I put my coffee cup back in the saucer with a faint chinking sound.

'There's something else, isn't there?' I said. 'Something you haven't told me.'

The girl inclined her head, the light shining on her soft blonde hair.

'I told you she was keeping bad company, Mr Faraday. She had a new boy friend lately. You may have heard of him. A man called Marcel Roco.'

CHAPTER TWO

1

Stella's pencil made a sudden scratching noise that seemed to tear a jagged hole in the atmosphere in here. I held Tina Matthews' eyes with my own.

'You mean the racketeer, Miss Matthews. If we're talking about the same person he's a professional hit man.'

The girl appeared to shrink in the chair.

'That's the one, Mr Faraday,' she said quietly. 'But perhaps you won't want to take the case now you know that.'

I grinned faintly.

'I didn't say so, Miss Matthews. I mix with a lot of racketeers in my business. It's just that I like to know what I'm getting into.'

I lit another cigarette and put the spent match-stalk in the earthenware tray on my desk.

'And you think Roco may have something to do with your sister's disappearance?'

Tina Matthews shrugged.

'It's possible, Mr Faraday. But of course, I don't know anything about his movements. I didn't dare mention his name when I phoned the club.'

'Very wise of you, Miss Matthews,' I said. 'We've got to tread softly here until we find out a little more about the situation.'

'Then you'll take the case, Mr Faraday.'

I stared at Stella for a few seconds, the cogs of my mind turning over without engaging in anything.

'I'm already on it, Miss Matthews. But I'll want to know a lot more about you and your sister before you leave this office.'

The girl looked from me to Stella and then back again.

'Of course, Mr Faraday. I'll tell you everything I know.'

'You have a photograph of your sister?' I

10

said. 'I'll need to see what she looks like.'

'I brought one of her professional shots with me. It's a small proof of one of the big studies they hang outside the club. But it's an excellent likeness.'

'I'm sure,' I said.

I waited while the girl fumbled in the small leather handbag she held awkwardly on her lap.

'Does Roco hang out around The Blue Parrot, Miss Matthews?' I said.

She shook her head, still struggling with the bag.

'I'm sure I don't know, Mr Faraday. But if you go there I expect someone on the staff could tell.'

I could see Stella's faint smile as she bent her head over the scratchpad. Like me she knew that co-operation from people in such places was pretty thin stuff. Those who run niteries don't like characters snooping around, particularly private operatives like me. But I didn't tell our client that.

She finished wrestling with her bag in the end and pushed a small square of card across the desk. I studied it carefully.

Though tiny, the shot was a good one, taken by a professional under professional lighting conditions. Erika Matthews looked quite a dish. She wore a fairly modestly cut evening gown and she was leaning on an ornamental pillar with an almost insolent nonchalance.

11

There was something about the lips, the eyes and the hair that uncannily echoed the girl in front of me.

'There's an astonishing likeness between the two of you,' I said.

Tina Matthews smiled.

'So I've been told, Mr Faraday. We were so much alike when young that people often mistook one for the other. If you know what I mean. When we got older we adopted different hair styles, which made things easier.'

I put the picture down on my blotter.

'So I should imagine. I'll hang on to this in the meantime.'

'Certainly, Mr Faraday. That's why I brought it.'

'There's nothing else you can think of that would assist?' I said.

Tina Matthews shook her head.

'Not offhand, Mr Faraday. I'm afraid you must think I'm being very unhelpful.'

'Not at all, Miss Matthews. Have you a phone number where we can reach you during the day?'

The girl nodded, her eyes mysterious and distant beneath the glaze of the big glasses. She would be pretty high-powered without them, I was thinking. I waited while she gave the number to Stella. The girl finished off her coffee and got up hesitantly.

'You've been very kind.'

'I haven't done anything yet,' I told her. 'But

you can rest assured I'll look into it.'

Her hand was cool and firm as she gave it to me to shake. There was the faint aroma of lavender water about her as she moved toward the door. Or something about that price range.

Then she seemed to recollect something, turned and went back to Stella, shaking hands in the same diffident way with her.

'You've both been most kind.'

She went out so quietly and unobtrusively it was like an elusive breeze passing through the office. The faint sound of the outer waiting room door closing was like an intrusion in the silence.

2

'Well, well,' Stella said. 'Straight out of Quality Street.'

I grinned and went to sit back at my desk.

'You can say that again,' I told her.

Stella came on over and sat down in the client's chair.

'She's too true to be good,' she said.

'You're prejudiced,' I said. 'She seemed pretty nice to me. And stop quoting Bernard Shaw.' Stella gave me one of her shuttered looks.

'I didn't know I was,' she said insincerely.

'What do you make of it, Mike?'

I shrugged.

'Seems a fairly ordinary sort of situation. Good girl out of her depth. Bad girl sister runs off with a hoodlum. It happens every day.'

Stella made a wry face.

'Not in my world, Mike.'

'You're different,' I said. 'But I go for the scenario I've just outlined.'

'You've been seeing too many old Warner Brothers movies on TV,' she said.

'Maybe,' I said. 'But it looks that way from where I'm standing.'

Stella still looked dubious.

'But even if she had gone off she would surely have contacted her sister, Mike. It doesn't make sense.'

Like always, she had a point.

'I'm listening,' I said.

Stella shrugged, crossing her legs in the client's chair in a way I always find unnerving.

'I've nothing against the girl, Mike. Don't think that. It's just that she's so unworldly it isn't true.'

I grinned through my cigarette-smoke that was wreathing its way slowly to the ceiling.

'There are still a few girls like it about. But she's right to be worried.'

'She's so unworldly she didn't offer you a fee,' Stella said.

'So she just forgot,' I said. 'It happens. She was plenty agitated underneath.'

'In which case her sister probably wrote her a letter which she's left unopened in her handbag,' Stella went on.

I looked at her through narrowed eyes.

'She must have been more attractive than I figured,' I said. 'She seems to have gotten under your skin.'

Stella smiled. It seemed to lighten up the whole office.

'So you did notice the woman behind the spectacles, Mike. All I'm doing is trying to point out a few possibilities.'

She got up and collected my empty cup.

'So you don't need my advice.'

'I didn't say that,' I told her. 'I'll always need your advice.'

Stella came around the desk and looked at me with very blue eyes.

'That's different. What's your first move?' I stared at her for a long moment.

'You know very well. There's only one place to go. The Green Parrot.'

'The Blue Parrot,' Stella corrected me patiently. 'That's my advice. You know what those sort of places are.'

'You mean carry a gun,' I said.

Stella nodded.

'That's exactly what I mean, Mike. That girl was even more agitated than appeared on the surface. Something bad could have happened over there.'

'It's good advice, honey,' I said. 'I intend to take it.'

I got up and we were still standing there

when there came a nervous tap and the waiting room door slowly opened. The fair head of Tina Matthews was framed in the opening.

'I'm so sorry, Mr Faraday. The question of a fee quite slipped my mind. I've written you a cheque. Would three hundred dollars for out of pocket expenses and so forth be all right to start with?'

'I'm sure it will be more than enough, Miss Matthews,' I said gravely.

I avoided Stella's eye.

'My Keeper of the Till will deal with it,' I said.

I went on out quickly before either of them could say anything. My smile lasted me all the way to the lobby.

CHAPTER THREE

1

It was late afternoon before I got over to The Blue Parrot. After lunch I'd taken Stella's advice and broken out the Smith-Wesson .38 from the small armoury I keep in a locked cupboard in the bedroom of my rented house over on Park West. It's a real man-stopper and I always felt well-dressed with it on difficult assignments.

Not that this promised to be difficult but

Stella's advice was pretty sound like always and the pressure of the piece in the nylon holster against my chest muscles as I tooled my five-year-old powder-blue Buick round the curves was reassuring.

It was cooler now and a welcome breeze had gotten up from somewhere. The shadows were long on the ground as I reached the section I wanted and pulled up at a red, studying the large-scale I had taped to the dashboard. I found it was the third intersection from where I was at and signalled right, boring across on to an uphill boulevard where the distant neon spelled out the title of the place. In blue lighting, of course.

The Blue Parrot was and is a fairly jazzy four-storey block of white stucco and Californian Spanish architecture with a roof of crab-tiles and lots of palms and tropical scenery that was doing nothing much but wilt this time of the afternoon.

There were several acres of shaved turf with sprinklers going and I tooled on down the façade to the parking lot, enjoying the freshness of the sprinklers and catching the cloying perfume of exotic flowers that looked like scarlet wounds against the greenness of the turf.

The place was open, like I figured, though there were only a dozen or so cars in the lot, probably belonging to early drinkers; or late-staying expense account lunchers. I pulled the

Buick in under the shade of some pepper trees and killed the motor. The sound of traffic from the boulevard beyond made a restless noise like the fretting of the sea.

I walked on up the long spiral entry that had a tesselated tile paving like something I'd seen in a colour brochure on Rio. It looked like the same artist had been employed on both jobs. My shadow was printed sharp and black on the dusty filing and I was glad to get in under the shade of the glass canopy over the entrance.

It was cool and dim in the marble-floored lobby and fans were going. I stopped for a moment, waiting for my eyes to adjust. On the far wall, between the tall bronze bracket lamps that broke the white façade at intervals were big colour photographs of artistes appearing in The Blue Parrot cabaret line-up. There was one of Erika Matthews all right.

I went on over and studied it carefully. It was a little more revealing than the print Tina had given me and which was now burning a hole in my wallet. She was singing at the piano this time, leaning against it, evidently in the middle of some blues number. The dark skirt was split and she was showing a generous expanse of thigh. From what I could see—and that was plenty—the legs were sensational.

I wondered vaguely how Tina Matthews would stack up against this beauty who was evidently dyed blonde when the shot was taken. They were sisters and maybe their vital statistics were similar. I gave up such thoughts in the end. It was too hot this afternoon.

I wandered over to another blue neon sign that was burning the dusk over a high doorway; that spelt out BAR-MEZZANINE and the long room inside was almost empty except for a few solitary drinkers scattered about the tables. No-one looked up as I came in and I walked over noiselessly on the thick carpet, conscious of the balcony beyond that fell to the dance floor and stage below; dark and silent now at this time of day.

There was a long horseshoe bar flanked by stools of blue leather and a melancholy-looking pug in a crumpled white jacket who was disturbing the beer-froth on the bar counter with a cloth. I figured he'd only started doing it when he saw me coming. I nodded pleasantly as I got up to him.

'Nice day,' I ventured.

He shrugged, looking round at the dim lighting. 'Is it?'

'Sure,' I said. 'If you can take my word for it.'

He bent to the bar surface, like it was the Field of the Cloth of Gold or something.

'Take it or leave it. You do want something to drink?'

I nodded, looking round the hushed interior. If this was where the action was I'd have hated to have been in the Central Library this afternoon. I ordered a carafe of Paul

Masson white and sat down on one of the stools before he could come back with any more of his lightning repartee.

It was a nice wine chilled, like always, and I savoured it in the long-stemmed glass the barman had provided. I didn't really want the whole carafe so I asked him to join me. He gave me a smile about three millimetres wide, pulling out another glass from under the bar.

'I can't be bribed, buddy,' he said in a hoarse growl.

I grinned.

'You must be one of the few honest and poor men around,' I said.

The barman shrugged, holding up his glass to the light.

'Your health.'

He drained the wine almost in one gulp, smacking his lips loudly.

'Say, this isn't bad.'

'You mean you never taste it?' I said.

He shook his head.

'I got to be careful in my business. But a couple of glasses this time of day won't do any harm. Though I wouldn't like my regulars to see me.'

'Be my guest,' I said.

He poured himself another, taking it more slowly this time. I noticed he had hard grey eyes. They didn't miss much beneath the casual manner.

He left his glass three-quarters filled and

went back along the bar, picking up his cloth routine where he'd left off.

'You didn't come in just for a drink, buddy,' he said after a bit.

I squinted at one of the wall lights through my glass. I was on my second now and feeling great.

'Not exactly,' I said.

He didn't say anything for a while, just kept working back down the bar toward me. I finished my second, left him the rest of the carafe. He gave me a little stiff bow as he re-filled his glass.

'Drop by every day,' he said.

'I thought you couldn't be bribed,' I told him. He cracked his face a little.

'I'm looking for Miss Matthews,' I said. 'Miss Erika Matthews.'

The pug-faced barman shrugged.

'Who's she?'

'She works here,' I said patiently. 'She's a singer in the cabaret.'

The barman re-distributed some of the beer and spirit suds round the top of the counter with his cloth.

'Yeah, well, I don't get to study or to know the talent out on the floor there. Some of them are pretty nice. But then again, some of them ain't.'

'I get your point,' I said. 'Can you tell me where I can find her?'

The barman pointed somewhere vaguely

over his shoulder.

'The dressing rooms are in back there. That ain't my domain. I guess you better see the manager.'

'Who might he be?' I said.

The barman went on re-distributing liquid like it was the thing he found most fascinating in the world.

'He might be almost anybody, bud,' he said studiedly. 'But his name happens to be Lancelot Green. It's unfortunate but true just the same.'

I put him down as a comic. He wasn't giving me anything but feed lines for the moment. He paused in his sud-pushing and looked at me sharply.

'But you'd best not get wandering around the corridors. You better see Green first. His office is the third on the right just beyond that green curtain there.'

I looked at him reflectively.

'This place should be called The Green Parrot,' I said.

I went on over toward the curtain before he could come back with anything else.

2

Behind the curtain was a flight of steps lit only by one shaded lamp at the head and a lot of stale air overlaid with the type of antiseptic perfume these sort of places use backstage. I went up the carpeted stairway two treads at a time, listening to the lonely pumping of the blood in my veins, conscious of the bulk of the Smith-Wesson in its harness against my chest muscles.

There was a faint thumping from the far distance that gradually resolved itself into an orchestra playing, with a lot of drum-beats beneath the melody. I guessed it was a hi-fi belonging to one of the staff playing somewhere behind one of the closed doors off the long corridor in which I found myself.

There was a glass panel hanging on chains from the ceiling whose inscribed gold lettering, illuminated from behind said: ARTISTES' DRESSING-ROOMS. It indicated a turn to the right so I went straight ahead down the anonymous-looking grey-painted corridor to another illuminated panel which spelt out: MANAGEMENT: PRIVATE. There were a lot of photographs and paintings of show-girls wearing little but goose-pimples and smiles hanging on the walls but I had no time for the decor this afternoon.

It was hot and airless in here and heat even seemed to leak out of the grey carpeting and up through the soles of one's shoes. The doors went on but there was nothing on them but various people's names; others led to toilets and store-rooms if the gold lettering on the door-panels meant anything. I reached the end of the run and found there was a T-junction.

The corridor went on like something out of an old Alan Ladd movie and there was another small stairway ahead with a landing at the top with several more doors. I went up the small stair, going quietly on the carpeting, walking on the balls of my feet. The sound of the hi-fi was distant now, almost inaudible amid the acres of carpet and hessian-covered walls.

I was halfway up the stair when two men came out of a doorway at the end of the passage facing me. One of them was a tall, lean man with blond hair, in his early forties, who had pro written all over him. It was the leading character who concerned me for the moment. Despite the heat he wore a dark suit with chalk-stripes that sat on him awkwardly, like his muscles were bursting through.

He had a blank, flat face; greasy black hair that was cut short and lay on the top of his flat skull like soot on the rim of a chimney-pot; and eyes the colour of dirty mud. If there can be such a thing.

For the rest he had a black string tie that looked like someone had thrown it at his grubby shirt front; and wall-to-wall shoulders. Altogether he was one of the nicest things I'd seen all week and as he cruised on down the corridor, his meaty arms seeming to touch the walls either side, he would have frightened the average insurance salesman half out of his wits. He wasn't doing much for my morale come to think of it.

He opened his rat-trap mouth half a millimetre.

'This is private through here, mister.'

'So I've been told,' I said.

The eyes were like icy mud now.

'You got business here?'

'I'm looking for Green,' I said.

The big man had paused now. The blond character was leaning against the wall farther down. I knew I could handle him all right, providing he wasn't carrying a piece.

'Mr Green to you, buddy.'

The big man spat the words out. He was stationary at the far end of the landing which gave me time to mount the rest of the stairs. I felt better then. I found he was head and shoulders shorter than me. I walked over to an alcove where a fire extinguisher was standing on a bracket fixed to the wall.

I leaned against it and smiled pleasantly at the two men.

'Mr Green, then.'

The big man's smile opened another quarter millimetre.

'What's your business?'

'Private,' I said.

The big man shook his head.

'You still can't see him.'

The blond man made a harsh, snorting

laugh back in his nostrils. He reminded of a horse on its hind legs. Except that horses are much nicer.

'Want to bet?' I said.

The big man moved fast then but he was still too slow. He was so wide he had to manoeuvre sideways a little. While he was doing that the blond man was out of sight. The big man's fist, looking like a side of beef in the dim light of the corridor, made a blurred impression in the air.

I'd made my move by then. I'd already got one hand under the extinguisher. My left had the handle and I brought the heavy metal canister over and slammed it into the side of the bouncer's head. He dived into the far wall with a crash that shook the building.

He was already cold before he disfigured the carpet. The blond man's eyes were narrowed as he reached into the front of his suit. I punched the button of the extinguisher then, got to the hose connection with my left. He screamed as the foaming chemicals caught his eyes. He went down clawing and moaning. I slammed him with the extinguisher, put him out fast.

I took the cannon from the blond man's pocket and covered that with foam too. I left the gadget squirting and gurgling away further down the corridor, keeping the stuff off my suit. No-one seemed to have heard the fracas, which was only slightly less disturbing than

World War Two.

There was a water cooler up the far end of the corridor. I got down there fast, came back with a plastic cup full of water. I bathed the blond man's eyes, dried his face off with his handkerchief. I wasn't in the blinding business. When I was satisfied that he'd maybe only have sore eyes for a few days I straightened up and examined the big man. He was breathing heavily through his nose. I figured both heavies would be out for an hour at least.

The Smith-Wesson made a heavy pressure against my chest as I went over to the door which said MANAGEMENT on it.

CHAPTER FOUR

1

I went on in without knocking, opening the door quietly and shutting it the same way. The key was in the lock and I turned it to make sure no-one surprised us. It was a big place and dim in keeping with the rest of The Blue Parrot so I needed a few seconds for my eyes to adjust. When I could see what was going on it was worth looking at.

It wasn't just the phoney stone fireplace and the expensive-looking water-colours on the walls; the brown velvet-lined walls themselves;

the leather-bound books on business law and California legislative procedures, surprising though these were; or even the intricately detailed nineteenth century ship models that marched down one side the big room, sailing through their glass cases, that made the place like a museum.

Any other time I might have been interested in all this. But not now. I could hear a faint noise that sounded like scratching or someone furtively moving around in the semi-darkness in here. There was just one lamp burning, near the fireplace. The light it was throwing off shone and flickered on faces that were moving and bobbing about in the blackness up the far side of the room.

They were dark, savage faces with deep eye-sockets and they reminded me of Indian carvings or photographs of Aztec masks that I'd once seen in a colour magazine. I had the Smith-Wesson out now and I held it up ready for use. I moved over quickly, my progress inaudible on the thick carpeting, keeping in rear of the ship models in the big cases.

I felt a faint crawling at the base of my spine. The faces were in a rough line, somewhere up near the ceiling. If people were wearing them they must have been about ten feet tall. I relaxed then. I might even have had a thin smile if there'd been a mirror around.

I guessed, even before I got there, that they were either papier-mâché or some other light material and were purely for decor. They were suspended on wires like mobiles and were simply moving around in the warm air. The light from the lamp was providing the rest of the effects.

I knew now this room was empty. My eyes had adjusted and the place had no occupants. But the bar-keep had implied that Green was in back. And the two plug-uglies I'd outed in the hall were obviously there to prevent unauthorised people from getting to Green. I could see now there were two mahogany doors in rear of the place. One of them was ajar and a thin shaft of light was spilling from underneath it.

The faint scratching noise went on and I knew it wasn't coming from the masks or anything to do with them. I got over to the doorway quickly. The sounds were louder. I'd wondered why Green had his quarters shuttered and curtained this time of the afternoon. I was wiser now.

I could see two-thirds of the apartment. It was got up as a study with lots more legal and other books in glass cases around. There were a couple of dim wall-lights burning and a big desk with a green leather top. I kept the Smith-Wesson ready for use while I made sure how many people were in the room. There were only two as it happened.

If the light in the outer office had been bizarre this was more natural. But just as sensational in its own way. Green was a pale-faced man of about thirty with black curly hair. He wore a pearl grey two-piece suit with a grey silk shirt and a blue bow-tie. That was in case anyone wanted to make notes for The Gentleman's Magazine. I didn't this afternoon. I was too busy watching the action.

There was a thin glaze of perspiration on Green's face and I could see a few beads on his trim black mustache. He was standing in front of the desk and keeping his hands busy. There was a tall blonde lying on top of the desk. Leastways, I guessed she would have been tall if she had been standing up. She wore little except a few sequins and she was squirming around.

It was the high heels of her shoes I could hear making the scratching noise against the leather surface of the desk. I leaned against the door jamb. This could have been an entertaining session except that my time was limited today. I was sorry to break up Green's play-time but I had some questions to ask.

The couple froze as I eased into the room, my shadow long in the glow of the wall-lamps. I smiled pleasantly at the dark man.

'Auditioning?' I said.

2

Green made a convulsive movement and for a

30

second I thought he was going to fall apart. The girl gave a startled cry and started up. The pale man's face was grey now. He pushed her back on to the desk, reached for a fur coat that was flung across a chair-back. He pulled it over the girl's naked shoulders with shaking fingers.

'What the hell do you want?'

His lips were trembling so much he could hardly get the words out.

'Just the answers to a few questions,' I said.

The girl gave another squeak. She was sitting up now, holding the coat together with her two hands. She was quite a looker.

'Beat it, Zelda,' Green said. 'We'll take this up later.'

He moved away, mopping his face with a red silk handkerchief he took from his breast pocket. He had his fingers inside the drawer before I moved around the desk and slammed it shut.

He gave a high, falsetto scream like a girl and blood came out the tips of his fingers.

'Naughty,' I said.

I cuffed him lightly across the face and he staggered back into a chair. He moaned, nursing his damaged fingers under his left armpit. The girl stared at me for a moment. I sensed rather than saw approval on her face.

'I've wanted to see that happen for a long time, mister,' she said.

I grinned.

'Now you've seen it. Best do as he says.'

31

She nodded and moved slowly away into the shadow. Presently I heard a door close in the silence. I opened up the drawer, took the Luger out of it. I held it up to Green. He sat with his eyes on the floor, tears streaming down his face.

'I suppose this is standard equipment recommended by the Nightclub Owners' Association?' I said.

His lips were twisted with pain and rage.

'Who are you? And what are you doing here? What do you want?'

I sat down on the edge of the desk, showed him the Smith-Wesson. It was rather like overkill but it had its effect.

'Rather a lot of questions for a naughty little man like you,' I said. 'But I'll answer them. The name's Faraday. I'm a private investigator. I can show you my licence details if you want to see them.'

He shook his head savagely and his lips were trembling again now. He took his hand out from under his armpit and studied the broken nails. His handkerchief was lying on the desk top and I passed it to him.

'Like I said I want the answers to a few questions,' I said. 'There was no need for gun stuff.'

'You came in with a gun,' he said sullenly.

'So I did,' I told him. 'I thought it advisable after a run-in with your goons in the corridor outside.'

'What happened to them?'

'They're sleeping it off,' I said. 'But we're getting away from the point.'

I shifted my position on the desk, raising the Smith-Wesson until it was aligned on his legs. He shifted away like he was expecting me to shoot any second. He was recovering himself now.

'I'll see you get bounced off your licence for this, Faraday,' he said thickly.

'It's been tried,' I said. 'But I'm still around. You asked me what I wanted. I'm looking for a girl called Erika Matthews. She works here, I understand.'

He shifted in the chair, adjusting the handkerchief round his shattered fingers, looking at me directly for the first time. They were dishonest, insincere eyes. I'd seen those sort of eyes on a lot of club owners and managers who were more used to sailing the wrong side of the law than the right. I'd been around L.A. too long to mistake the expression.

'Sure, she works here,' he said in a voice so low I had a job to catch it. 'A lot of girls work here.'

'I can imagine,' I said.

I looked around the room, taking in the detail. There was a lot of stuff that looked like erotic art on the walls. When I'd examined them more closely I could see they were professionally shot colour photographs, from the life. I recognised the blonde girl in one of them.

'Erika's sister's getting worried about her,' I said. 'She hasn't been home lately. I'd like to know where she's at.'

Green stirred in the chair, made a movement like he was going to get up. I waved him down again with the Smith-Wesson barrel. While he was thinking up his answer I hooked the Luger over, broke out the shells.

'That's just so we shan't have any accidents,' I said.

Green licked dry lips.

'How should I know where Erika Matthews is?' he said. 'These girls come and go.'

I shook my head.

'Try again, sonny. Erika Matthews is one of your star attractions. She doesn't just come and go. Or do you leave the booking of the cabaret artistes to your Director of Artistic Studies?'

Green looked pained. And not only because of his injured hand. I had a sudden thought then. 'You are Lancelot Green?'

'Sure I am, Faraday. It's a name you won't forget in a hurry.'

'You have a point,' I said. 'But we were talking about Erika Matthews. I'm still waiting for your reply.'

'You'll get nothing out of me,' he said quickly.

I looked at him. There were two red spots

34

burning on his cheekbones.

'You're not very good at this, sonny,' I said. 'If you have got something to hide you'd better make with the verbiage. I can easily get the boys in blue in. Or would you like me to start on your other hand?'

He gave a sudden start and shoved his left under his right armpit. He was a ludicrous sight. I figured he was in the wrong business. Or maybe a front for someone. A manager, possibly, keeping the store for an undisclosed owner. That was generally the situation. I lifted the Smith-Wesson but we were interrupted. It was the girl Zelda's voice, strained and tense from the darkness at the edge of the room.

'Excuse me, mister. Lance? Can I have my clothes, honey?'

I grinned at the dark man's expression. He was making little gurgling noises in back of his throat as I got up and came toward him. I went around him, found the girl's tangle of clothing in a big easy chair. I made a bundle of them and hefted them in the direction of the blonde number's voice.

'Thanks, mister. You're a gentleman.'

I grinned again.

'That makes two of us.'

I went back to Green, put the Smith-Wesson barrel against the back of his neck. I waited for him to come down from the ceiling.

'My patience is running thin,' I said. 'Now we get the answers.'

CHAPTER FIVE

1

'I came here to make a simple inquiry,' I said. 'You've mounted a big production over it. What's the story?'

Green's face was turning the same colour as his name. He gulped and fiddled with the handkerchief covering his injured fingers.

'No production,' he said. 'This is a private club. We don't like guys like you busting in.'

I held up the Smith-Wesson close to his face. He squirmed away.

'You'd better get used to it,' I said. 'I'm not leaving here until I get those answers.'

Green shrugged, his eyes smouldering in the dim light of the lamps.

'Erika Matthews? Sure, she works here. Her face is plastered all over outside.'

'So?' I said.

He shrugged again.

'She didn't show up one night. We put on a replacement. She's on a month's vacation so far as I know. That was the story we got.'

'From whom?' I said.

Green moved over cautiously in the chair, out of direct range of the Smith-Wesson barrel. I lowered it toward the floor. I was playing this character along. Looked like I might strike gold if I had enough time with him.

'I asked you a question.'

Green made a little strangled noise back in his throat.

'Why don't you go ask her agent?' he said. It was my turn to shrug.

'Maybe I will. But I'm asking you.'

Green's eyes were turned toward the floor now. I could see the places on the carpet where the blood dripping from his injured fingers had made little dark stains on the carpet. They were the same colour as his eyes at the moment.

'We had a phone call. From her agent as far as I know. I didn't take the message personally. He said she'd been taken sick. She asked if she could bring her vacation forward. We had no option but to agree. We put a printed notice outside the club. I guess she'll be back inside the next week.'

'You're asking me to believe that?' I said.

Green lifted his head.

'Take it or leave it, Mr Faraday. It's the truth.'

'I can easily check it,' I said.

'Suit yourself,' Green said.

'He got a name?' I asked.

Green nodded.

'It's Leroy. It's in the book.'

'I'll find it,' I said.

I gave him a long, steady look. He was squirming on the chair now. He was the most uneasy man I'd ever seen.

'You ask me to believe she'd go off without contacting her sister.'

Green made a low groaning sound. I figured he was either exasperated or his fingers were paining him again.

'I'm not asking you to believe anything, Mr Faraday. I'm just telling you the plain truth. Why not go see Leroy?'

'I might just do that,' I said.

I was thinking up the next piece of dialogue when there came a hammering on the door of the outer office that seemed to make echoing vibrations off the walls in here.

2

I grinned at Green, lifting the Smith-Wesson barrel slightly. A faint voice was audible now.

'You all right, Mr Green? We got a crazy guy in the club.'

'That makes two,' I said. 'Tell them.'

Green opened his mouth. A quavering noise came out.

'You'll have to do better than that,' I said. 'Tell them it's all right.'

Green cleared his throat, gave me a despairing look.

'Everything's all right,' he called.

The door handle was tried then and a mumbling dialogue began. I rammed the barrel of my piece into the club-manager's gut. I thought he was going to throw up. His voice had the desperate bellow of a stud bull in heat. Or something along those lines.

'Everything's okay! Beat it!'

The noise at the door stopped. I got up from the desk and backed quickly away from Green. I could hear footsteps now, then a sharp clatter. I guessed someone was moving the fire extinguisher. I buttoned the study light, bringing everything in the place up in a harsh glare. I stood looking down at the girl's stockings and the black suspender belt that lay on the chair cushion.

'I didn't know they'd come back in,' I said.

Green licked his lips.

'This won't get you anywhere, Faraday. There's ways of conducting an inquiry.'

'Sure,' I said. 'Except that you boys started it first.'

The dark man gave a smile that reminded me of a ferret which suddenly sees its supper appear in front of it. Not that I'm very much up on ferrets. But that was the general idea. Green got up then.

He was still nursing his fingers but he had a sort of dignified defiance about him. It didn't command respect but I had a faint flicker of sympathy for him. I tossed it out the window before it could grow.

'You have still to get out of here, Mr Faraday.'

'Don't be childish,' I said. 'You're coming with me. If there's any trouble you get it first.'

Green stared at me like he was coming out of a trance. I guessed this sort of scene was alien to his life-style. He had goons to handle the gritty end. I rammed the Smith-Wesson back into his stomach.

'Just move,' I said. 'We don't want any trouble do we?'

He licked his lips.

'We've had enough for one day, Mr Faraday.'

'That's right,' I said. 'And if you do hear from Miss Matthews, you will ring me, won't you? I'm in the book.'

The pale face was set now.

'You'll be hearing from us, Mr Faraday,' he said viciously.

I grinned.

'Now walk. And remember my reflexes are pretty good. I wouldn't want anything bad to happen to you on the way out.'

I put the Smith-Wesson in my pocket, let him feel the muzzle in his side. He moved over toward the door like he'd been stung. Seemed to me he was in the wrong business for a man with his delicate nerves. I thumbed back the automatic catch on the door.

'You will be careful, won't you,' I said.

He swallowed heavily.

'I'll be careful, Mr Faraday.'

We went out in the corridor. It seemed to be

full of people. There were a couple of showgirls with spangles and feathers stuck in strategic places and two men in coveralls. Green's heavies had been moved but there was some blood on the wall and two more durable-looking men were stationed at the end of the corridor.

The two men in coveralls were sponging up the foam made by the extinguisher.

'What the hell . . .' Green began.

'We had a little fire drill,' I said. 'It's recommended by the licensing authority for clubs like this.'

We walked on down the corridor. The two big men in dark suits moved to block the way.

'It's all right, boys,' Green said in a trembly voice. 'Mr Faraday is just leaving.'

The two frosty faces with the corrugated iron foreheads relaxed.

'Just a little misunderstanding, boys,' I said. 'No hard feelings.'

The two drew back either side the corridor. I pulled Green by the arm. I smiled at the couple.

'I don't think so,' I said. 'Go on ahead.'

The two goons looked at Green. I could feel him trembling clear down to his socks.

'Do like Mr Faraday says.'

The couple shrugged. They turned and walked away very stiffly, leaning forward on the balls of their feet. We went down the staircases and back into the main bar again. I made Green go ahead of me through the curtain but there was no-one there. The two goons had gone up the far end of the bar but their eyes didn't miss much.

The bar-keep was still carrying out his mopping operations.

'You found Mr Green all right?' he said morosely.

'Looks like it,' I said. 'He was very informative, like you said.'

Green turned to face me. His eyes looked dark and haunted.

'This is where I leave you, Mr Faraday.' I shook my head.

'I think not, Mr Green. You're my insurance for the moment. We'll go take a little ride.'

I almost laughed out loud at his reaction to this corny old cliché but this was no time for it. I caught him by the arm again and almost carried him out the club. He was like a jelly. I wondered who he was fronting for. A creep like this couldn't keep a chorus line in order, let alone a few tough boys like I'd seen around. It was an interesting question but one I couldn't hope to go into this afternoon.

We went out into the dazzling sunlight, shading our eyes against the sudden glare.

'It's still daylight,' I said. 'One loses all count of time in there.'

I stared into Green's ashen face.

'You really ought to take more exercise.'

I almost dragged him across to my heap,

rammed him down into the passenger seat, putting the door catch into the lock position before slamming it home. There was no-one around as I tooled the Buick on out. Green faced ahead, his eyes down on his toes.

'What do you intend to do with me, Mr Faraday?'

'Maybe use you to prop up a motorway junction, Mr Green,' I said. 'I haven't decided yet. But like I told you, you're in the wrong business. You mustn't come unglued just because a private operative asks a few awkward questions. So there's got to be more. Right?'

Green shook his head violently but I could see that I'd struck home. There was no point in scaring the daylights out of him any longer. He was beginning to nauseate me. And I'm a character it's difficult to do that to. I spend so much time in garbage and turning over the seedy underbelly of life. I found a slot in the traffic, signalled and drew the Buick into the kerb. Green looked at me white-faced.

'Get out,' I said. 'The walk back will do you good. It's probably the only normal exercise you'll get this year.'

Green was still nursing his fingers, started to give me a venomous look, then thought better of it.

'You'll be hearing from us.'

'Just make sure you keep in touch,' I said.

I leaned over and unlocked the door for

him. He got out and stood looking in at me, still trembling.

'You can get back to your hobbies now,' I said. I was still laughing when I reached the other side of town.

CHAPTER SIX

1

Alex Leroy's offices were in a fairly upbeat section and I got over there long before closing hours though it took me some while to park and I had to walk a couple of blocks back. Which meant I was nice and hot and dusty by the time I hit his place. It was dim in the lobby and it took me a moment or two to adjust my eyes to read the gold-painted signs on the board that gave the locations of the offices in the five-storey building.

There was no elevator and Leroy was located on the fourth floor. It figured. There was no-one around in the bare lobby with its filed floor and antiseptic walls so I guessed the ground floor housed offices too. I found out later that the whole building was devoted to movie and theatrical agents of one sort or another.

I say theatrical but they were really people who sold live entertainment to casinos, clubs, road-houses and such-like. Though there was still a lot of live theatre with name players in California, it was mostly handled by the New York boys. Who tended to stay off-Broadway.

I walked up a couple of flights and then rested on the landing. Not that I was tired but I needed a cigarette and a little time to think over a couple of factors. Green's had been such an extraordinary performance that one could read quite a lot into it. It didn't look too good from Erika Matthews' point of view.

I had a gut-feeling about it. One's seldom wrong on such things. I figured something had happened to her. Green may not have known exactly but he had a good idea. That was why he was running scared. The agent might know more. My bet was Roco but I didn't want to tip my hand there yet. Like I said I had to feel my way carefully.

And I was convinced Tina Matthews might know a little more than she'd told me. Not that I thought she was insincere. Her concern for her sister was genuine enough. Perhaps she suspected what might have happened. But she could be scared too. I shouldn't forget that. And a woman was far more vulnerable than a man.

Green was in something up to his eyeballs. My guess he was more scared of Roco than of me. And maybe the employees at the club were goons in Roco's pay. There were a lot of interesting possibilities. And if I hung in there long enough I'd start getting feedback. Like always in the form of blackjacks, balled fists and the occasional lead greeting card.

I grinned at my reflection in a dusty mirror that was screwed to the wall on the second floor landing and started to gumshoe my way up to the third. I could hear the thin pecking of typewriters now, strained through flimsy wall partitions; plywood doors and the hot, stale atmosphere in here.

I'd been keeping my eye on the black-painted legends on the frosted-glass panels of the offices I'd been passing and they were like the ground floor board said. All agents of one sort or another; mostly the other. I wondered how they made out; more to the point, how their clients made out. Apart from the top-liners, most of the artistes at any rate, were in a more hopeless profession than I was.

Lives of quiet desperation, Mike, I quoted to myself. I went up from the third landing to fourth. It was quieter here and the people behind these doors must be using quill pens. The joke lasted me all of three yards. I went on down to the far end of the corridor, reading off the names on the doors to left and right.

I got to Alex Leroy's place in the end. It was just his name on the door with the legend: Agent beneath in Gothic script. I wasn't used to modesty in show business and I stared at it for a long second. Then I put my fingers on the door-handle, conscious of the pressure of the Smith-Wesson against my chest.

I eased on round the jamb, blinking in the bright light that came in from the large windows. It was just one big room with a railed-in enclosure on the left-hand side, with a desk; presumably for Leroy's secretary. There was no-one there now so I guessed she'd maybe stepped out. There was a bigger desk with a chair set in front of the biggest window so I guessed that would be for Leroy. There was no-one there either.

I went on in anyway, closing the door softly behind me. There was a small door on the right-hand side of the room, almost in the corner; it probably led to a cloakroom or an annexe and Leroy or his secretary had stepped out there for a minute. I got over to the desk and stood admiring the decor and the California atmosphere.

There was a comfortable leather chair in front of the desk and I sat down in it. I set fire to a cigarette and put the spent match-stalk in a crystal tray on a corner of the desk. There was a whole heap of documents on it and both the in and out trays were full so I guessed maybe Leroy was a pretty busy man. When he was around, that is.

I sat there for perhaps ten minutes, studying the decor, smoking the cigarette, the wheels of my brain turning aimlessly around. There were a lot of first-class photographs in good frames on the walls, of fairly prominent artistes, so I guessed Leroy was in a pretty good line of business. I recognised Dean Martin in his younger days, doing a cabaret act in what seemed like a Las Vegas casino. The audience looked as if they were wearing mink underwear so I figured it was Las Vegas all right.

I was still sitting there fumigating the upholstery and resting my mind when the door in back opened and a tall, bald-headed man with a worried expression came out.

2

I was getting quite a few jittery people on Tina Matthews' case though I must admit this character made a more favourable impression. I got up to meet him as he hurried over.

'There didn't seem to be anyone around,' I said. 'So I came on in.'

He nodded absent-mindedly, his sharp brown eyes stabbing about the room.

'I'm afraid I haven't been able to book any spots for you yet, Mr Murray. I couldn't contact the circuit manager.'

I shook my head.

'I'm not Murray. My name's Faraday and show business isn't my scene.'

The tall, bald man looked at me anxiously. Then he held out his hand hesitantly. He wore a loose-fitting lightweight grey suit with a mauve coloured bow-tie that made it look like a tropical butterfly had suddenly alighted beneath his chin. I was getting a lot of bow-ties on this case. I figured they must be coming back in. The bald man puffed his cheeks in and out a few times like his breathing was troubling him.

'You are Alex Leroy?' I said.

He finished pumping my hand and moved around his desk, squinting at the sunlight that flooded through the big window in rear.

'Sure, I'm Leroy,' he said. Sorry we got our wires crossed, Mr Faraday. I was expecting Murray, the human fly. I've been trying to get him some bookings.'

He shrugged and looked at me reflectively. 'Show business!'

'I know how you feel,' I said. 'I get that way myself sometimes.'

Leroy sat back at his desk and fixed me with his brown eyes.

'My secretary Corinne's off sick today, Mr Faraday. It plays hell with my schedules. I got to do everything myself.'

He opened up a silver box on his desk and rooted around. He came up with a cigar that made Churchill's war-time Havanas look like toothpicks.

'Would you like one? Or do you prefer cigarettes.'

'I'll stick to my own,' I said. 'But thanks just the same.'

Leroy went through the usual ritual, removing the band, rubbing the weed around in his fingers and piercing it before lighting up and sending a cloud of pungent blue smoke toward the ceiling.

'What's your business, Mr Faraday?'

I grinned.

'I'm a private dick. I'm making a few inquiries about a client of yours. I wondered if you could help me.'

The eyes were narrowed now.

'Oh. What makes you think that, Mr Faraday?'

'Logic,' I said. 'It's perfectly simple. I was recommended to you by a Mr Green. He manages The Blue Parrot night spot. But you must know that. Your client works for him.'

It may have been my imagination but I thought a faint trembling ran along Leroy's massive cigar. A few specks of grey ash floated down and landed on the surface of the desk.

'Who might she be, Mr Faraday?'

I gave him another selection of my teeth.

'You just gave yourself away, Mr Leroy. You know as well as I do that Erika Matthews is your client. She plays cabaret at The Blue Parrot. Why be so coy about it?'

There were red spots starting out on the agent's cheeks now but his voice was even enough.

'There's no need to feel like that, Mr Faraday. I have to be diplomatic in my business. Of course Miss Matthews is my client. There's no secret about it. Though Green himself isn't my favourite person.'

'You have something there,' I said.

I rather liked Leroy. He had honesty and integrity in his bearing and manner. But there was something eating him. Several times his eyes flickered about the room during our conversation like he was expecting something bad to happen. I shifted my chair around unobtrusively, a little to the left so that I could see the entrance door over my shoulder.

Leroy leaned forward at the desk, the cigar steady in his hand again now.

'What's the problem, Mr Faraday?'

'It's Miss Matthews,' I said. 'She's gone missing, apparently. No-one knows where she is.'

Leroy's face cleared. He snorted and stared at me steadily.

'That's nonsense, Mr Faraday! She rang me a while back and said she was feeling sick. I arranged with The Blue Parrot to bring her vacation forward. She went up to Lake Arrowhead. I had a card from her there just a fortnight ago.'

'That I'd like to see,' I said.

Leroy spread his hands wide on the blotter.

'No problem, Mr Faraday,' he said cheerfully. 'It went to my private address. I'll bring it in in a day or two.'

I looked at him thoughtfully.

'I'd like that,' I said again. 'But it was the same story Green told me. It rings too pat.'

There were corrugated lines in Leroy's forehead as he leaned forward at the desk, twining the slim fingers of each hand together.

'I don't follow you, Mr Faraday.'

I sighed.

'It's very simple, Mr Leroy. Erika Matthews lived with her sister Tina Matthews. She left their apartment without saying a word to her sister. The sister hasn't heard a word from her since. And she's half out of her mind with worry.'

Leroy's mouth was compressed into a thin, tight line.

'It sounds ridiculous. But I could see how it would distress the sister.'

His voicc seemed worried.

'Not even a postcard?'

I shook my head.

'Not even a postcard.'

'I'd like to help you, Mr Faraday. But the card didn't indicate any hotel. I gathered Erika intended to move around a little. She hadn't taken a vacation for over two years. She had it coming.'

He frowned down at his blotter.

'Why didn't Tina contact me?'

I shrugged.

'She rang the club and was told Erika had left. I gather there were notices outside saying her performances were off. Her pictures are still outside so I guess they're expecting her back.'

The agent's mouth relaxed. The sun outside the windows made a shimmering moonscape of his bald pate.

'There you are then, Mr Faraday.'

'It won't do, Mr Leroy,' I told him. 'According to my client she wouldn't have gone off like that. Without a word. Or any letter or phone call since.'

The brown eyes were suddenly bleak.

'You think something may have happened to her?'

'It's possible,' I said. 'Anything's possible.'

Leroy suddenly became brisk, though I could sense the strain beneath his somewhat casual façade.

'You say you're a detective, Mr Faraday. You mind showing me your authority?'

'I wondered when you'd ask,' I said.

I got out the photostat of my licence in the leather wallet and passed it over to him. He studied it in silence, his eyes narrowed like the sunlight bouncing off the paper was blinding him.

'That's all right, Mr Faraday. I hope you didn't mind me asking?'

I took the wallet back and put it in my pocket.

'Not at all. You've never met me before. You have a right to see my credentials.'

Leroy sat back at his desk, fixing his gaze up

53

on the ceiling.

'Just how can we take this any further?' he said.

'There is one thing,' I told him.

I stopped. His eyes were fixed over my shoulder now. They had incredulity and terror in them. I glanced back toward the door. I was looking the wrong way. Something stirred at my right side and the roof fell in. I went out like cloche hats.

CHAPTER SEVEN

1

There was pain and noise and darkness. Plus a jolting that gave me nausea. When I came around I found I was looking at my feet. Like always, my shoes were scuffed. I was in an automobile because my nostrils had already caught the faint pungency of gasoline. The vehicle was stationary now, possibly at traffic lights because neons were shining down into the interior. That was why I was able to see my shoes.

I must have passed out again then because the next time things came into focus we were in darkness, going uphill. There were two men with me; one a big character, who was on the rear passenger seat at my side. He was probably the character who'd sapped me in Leroy's office. I remembered that much. He must have come out the cloakroom to my right. Which meant he'd been in there with the agent before I arrived. That was why Leroy had been so nervous during the interview. Maybe he'd been threatened. Or was part of the set-up.

I started pasting my thoughts together, the metal slicing bars that were beating tunes on my skull, gradually fading into silence. There was no sound now but the tuneless humming of the wheelman and the soft revolutions of the motor. A fresh breeze was blowing through the open driving window, bringing salt with it. We were going along a shore road then.

The blinds were down in rear so I couldn't see properly. I wondered again about Leroy. I'd like the answer to my question. He'd impressed me as being on the level with his story about Erika Matthews. I'd maybe ask him. If I got out of this. It depended on the correct sequence of events.

If Green had phoned Leroy and told him I was coming and then sent a couple of his heavies, Leroy was in up to his eyebrows. But Green may have contacted someone else. In which case I was on my way to an interview. None of this stuff made any sense. It depended on what Erika Matthews had been mixing in over at The Blue Parrot. It had to be pretty powerful stuff to get Green so agitated over a few innocuous questions from an obscure private eye.

I couldn't carry it any further and my head was hurting again so I gave it up. I felt a hand then. It was a powerful hand with fingers like steel claws. But the strength was held in reserve. In a grip surprisingly gentle, it pushed me back on the seat.

'You're round, then. You got a pretty good skull, Faraday.'

'So I've been told,' I said.

I swivelled to take in the man sitting next me. He had snow-white hair and a gentle, reflective face. Only the mouth gave him away; and the wariness of the eyes. The features could have belonged to a high-powered businessman; an industrial magnate; or the head of some big syndicate. Instead, he was a professional hit-man who'd made an art of his calling; and big business out of the proceeds.

He could have been on the board of Standard Oil; or one of the heads of MCA. In that atmosphere I wouldn't have picked him out from anyone else.

'Was Leroy in on this?' I said.

The face was wry, amused now. The tall man in the dark suit shook his head.

'Leave him out of it, Mr Faraday. He was just a frightened little man worried about his client. I just used his wash-room for half an hour, that's all.'

'Glad to leave him,' I said. 'I was just

curious. But you spoke in the past tense. Does that mean you took him out.'

The man on my right gave a soft laugh. His teeth were very white and even. He looked extraordinarily handsome then. I realised he couldn't have been more than fifty at the outside.

'Give me more credit than that, Mr Faraday. What do you take us for.'

'High grade professionals,' I said.

The wheelman made an ironical little bow in the direction of the rear-mirror.

'You're good, Mr Faraday.'

'Let's hope it stays that way,' I said. 'Mind if I smoke?'

'Not at all,' the man next me said cordially.

I got out my pack and he lit the cigarette for me with a silver lighter. His face was confident and relaxed in the dim, flickering light of the flame. He knew I had nothing else to reach for except cigarettes. I'd already checked, as a matter of routine; the Smith-Wesson had gone, of course.

'You mind telling me where we're going?' I said.

'We'd rather not say,' the wheelman said. 'But it's a real nice place. A beach-house farther up the bay.'

I feathered out blue smoke through my nostrils, watching moonlight stippling the ruffled surface of dark water now.

'I'm in need of a vacation,' I said.

The man next me shook his head.

'It's not a vacation, Mr Faraday. A business meeting, let's say.'

'You want to tell me about it?' I said.

The white-haired man shook his head again.

'Not at the moment, Mr Faraday. It's not our place. Our principal will let you know in due time.'

'And the subject of our meeting?' I said. I grinned in the darkness.

'I suppose that's restricted information too.'

'He'll tell you himself,' the white-haired man said.

The car drew up with a crunch in a gravelled driveway and in the blanched moonlight I could make out the outline of a long, low, Spanish-style house. I threw away the butt of my cigarcttc as wc got out.

2

The sedan growled off somewhere into the shadowy driveway. I walked slightly in front of the white-haired man. His face looked as finely chiselled and as emotionless as a bronze statuette in the moonlight. I didn't try anything. Not only was I not in the right condition but I knew the man next to me could drop me before I could make an inch in his direction.

He knew that I knew, of course. That was

why he hadn't found it necessary to say anything. We were both professionals. And I'd caught enough of his style to know that he was one of the most deadly characters I'd ever met.

His sapping me had proved that. He'd covered Leroy's office without me hearing him come before it had been too late. And the job he'd done on me had been calculated to a nicety. He'd dropped me with minimum force. He'd put me out for something like an hour.

Long enough for him to move me under cover of darkness. But not long enough to do any real damage or to have me unfit for questioning by his principal. Such men were rare. And they commanded a high price.

My brain was working again properly now. I knew then that this character was nothing to do with Green. He wouldn't work for such a man in a hundred years. So there was someone with far more clout behind this.

Which was interesting in itself. And involved something other than the simple disappearance of a little cabaret singer. I didn't bother to question the tall man. I knew I wouldn't get anything out of him. And I'd learn soon enough anyway. I had a momentary attack of giddiness and stopped.

The white-haired man seemed to know instinctively. He didn't alter his pace but his steel fingers were suddenly beneath my arm. He held me effortlessly; firmly but courteously, until the attack had passed.

'I'm sorry,' I said.

'Think nothing of it,' he said gently. 'I regretted the necessity. But you were too dangerous to treat otherwise.'

I stared up at the fat, bland moon riding high in the sky, gilding the wavetops down below. We were on a bluff up here and the house fell to its own private beach. I didn't bother to take in too much detail.

Either the house would be rented and no-one here if I ever came back. Or I wouldn't be in any condition to come back, which made the whole question of its location academic.

'Can you go on?'

'I'm fine,' I said.

The hand stayed within a few inches of my elbow as I went forward. I felt better now but some instinct warned me to play on it a little. To make out I was rather more beat-up than this character figured. It might come in useful later. I made my living by small details like this. And I kept on living the same way.

We were up near the entrance of the big Spanish-style bungalow now and the porch-light went off.

The white-haired man had my arm again.

'You will be very discreet when you see my principal, Mr Faraday. It could be extremely dangerous otherwise.'

I gave a cracked laugh. It sounded pretty feeble even to me.

'I'll behave,' I told him. 'I'm in no condition

to do anything else.'

I dragged my feet a bit as we went up on the stoop. The porch was dark now like I said but the white-haired man reached around me and opened the door. I went into a hall which smelt warm and dusty, like it hadn't been opened to the fresh air for a long time.

The tall man pushed me gently in front of him down a long corridor to where a crack of light showed from beneath the far door. I felt his hand under my elbow again. He kept behind me as I opened up the door on his instructions.

I blinked in the sudden light from a ceiling fixture and a standard lamp the far side of the room. There was nothing in the place but a lot of dusty air. I knew then I was right. The place was either rented or else used mainly for week-ends or holidays; shut up most of the year.

The furniture was of good quality but anonymous; the wallpaper faded and a little grubby in places; the carpet luxurious but neglected. There were chesterfields scattered about; a sideboard with bottles on a silver tray; and the obligatory stone fireplace. Some not very good prints filled up the odd spaces on the walls.

The white-haired man dragged over a heavy chair from the wall and put it down in the centre of the room.

'Sit down, Mr Faraday,' he said in the same

kindly, gentle voice he'd used throughout.

It sounded like I was coming for a job interview. I did like he said, fumbling around in my pocket for my cigarettes again. White-hair shook his head.

'I shouldn't, Mr Faraday. My principal wouldn't like it.'

'Bad for the health, is it?'

'Something like that,' he said.

I tried a grin, felt it might fall clear off my face. My head was aching again now and I sagged back in the chair like I was exhausted. It wasn't far from the truth.

'Your principal sounds a very fastidious man,' I said.

The man in the dark suit nodded.

'He is, Mr Faraday,' he assured me.

He went quietly back toward the door through which we'd come in and stood with his back to it. His restraint was far more deadly and impressive than if he'd been the blustering type. Now that I could see him in the light he seemed far less benevolent than he'd appeared in the car.

The hammered bronze face made a startling contrast to his snow-white hair. I hadn't caught the colour of his eyes for some reason. There was silence in the place for a bit. I used the interval to give the apartment the once-over. There were two exits to the big living room.

One was the door we'd used. There was another up the far end which might or might not lead to a bedroom. The blank, fireplace wall was to the right. To the left was a pair of large French windows that occupied perhaps a third of the wall space. I saw then that they were of unusual design.

Instead of being in two wings they had four, obviously folding back to give access to a terrace on summer evenings; the lock in the centre was strong enough but the bolts securing the wings were just ordinary things; not particularly massive, not particularly flimsy. It was something to remember.

I could hear a clock now. Its monotonous ticking was eroding the edges of the silence. I passed the time by trying to locate the sound. It showed how quiet it was up here; there wasn't even the faint beat of surf from the edge of the Pacific where the beach began below the garden. The house was ideal for the purpose white-hair's principal had chosen.

I couldn't hear any sound from the car either. I knew the wheelman had taken it farther down the drive. I hoped he'd turned it around by now. All this information could be useful in emergency.

I tried to work out the position of everything. I went over in my mind the route we'd taken inside the front door. I had it fixed firmly in my consciousness. The French windows faced the front garden and it was about a hundred feet across the lawn to the driveway where the car was parked.

I'd play it by ear after that. Assuming any of this scenario ever came about. I'd got the clock now. It was a big cased job standing in the shadow of the curtain at the far side of the French windows.

They weren't screened from the garden; there was nothing but gauze and the glass separating the room from the outside. That proved the place was isolated; probably the bungalow was the only one on this section of road. And it was high up on a shelf of rock so that no-one could look in unless they came up from the grounds.

I guessed then the rooms facing the beach would be the other side the corridor. A lot of people didn't like too much sun in their rooms. So they'd favour a more shady living room like here. End of inventory, Faraday, I told myself.

The white-haired man kept silence and there was no sign of the wheelman. I glanced surreptitiously at my watch. Already, twenty minutes had passed since we'd come in here. It was a great way to spend an evening.

I leaned back in the chair and focused up on the grandfather clock when there came the heavy vibration of footsteps from beyond the far door.

CHAPTER EIGHT

1

It opened and a tall, hard-looking man with blond hair cut en brosse came through. He wore a lightweight two-piece suit of a houndstooth pattern and morocco leather shoes that displayed a dazzling patina as he walked down the room toward us. He gave the white-haired man a bleak smile, revealing strong yellow teeth.

'Any trouble?'

White-hair shook his head.

'Everything went off according to routine.'

The tall man rubbed his hands briskly together, ignoring my presence. I was just a piece of furniture to him. He went over to fetch himself another chair with heavy leather arms and back.

He climbed up on it and sat with his feet on the cushion, resting his body on the broad upholstered back. From there he could dominate the whole room. I kept my eyes down. The back of his chair was about three feet from the rear of one of the big leather divans that made up a U-pattern in front of the fireplace. That could be useful information too.

The blond man stared at me unblinkingly

for about a minute. He gave me a brief, tight smile. 'Mr Faraday. Good of you to come.'

'You mean I had a choice?' I said.

The blond man exchanged a glance I couldn't read with the man at the door.

'Unfortunately, no. Necessity drives us all at times.'

'Mr Green has a loose mouth,' I said. 'He struck me as a pretty jittery character.'

The blond man stared at me expressionlessly. His eyes were a strange shade of blue. They reminded me of those glass eyes they have on children's dolls. I knew I was in the presence of a very dangerous man. White-hair hadn't exaggerated.

'Mr Green will be disciplined, Mr Faraday,' the hard-faced man said. 'You have made no mistake with his character. But then you are a professional, like ourselves.'

'We both have reputations, Mr Roco,' I said. 'It is Mr Roco, isn't it?'

There was a long silence in the room. Roco was still staring at me in what was meant to be an unnerving way. I traded him glance for glance until he had to speak.

'You have no doubt seen my photograph in the papers, Mr Faraday,' he said softly.

'Sure,' I said. 'They don't do you justice.'

Roco took his eyes off my face and examined his nails meticulously.

'We have something of a problem here, Mr Faraday,' he said at last. 'I'd like you to help us if you could.'

'I'm always willing to oblige,' I told him. He gave a stiff inclination of the head.

'That's an attitude I always admire, Mr Faraday. I heard you were around at the club inquiring after Erika Matthews. Would you care to elaborate on that?'

I shrugged.

'There's no secret about it. Her sister Tina Matthews hired me to find out what had happened to Erika. She hadn't been seen for some while and Tina was getting worried. She hadn't written or phoned in that time though she normally went home every night.'

Roco suddenly drew his breath in with an ugly sucking sound and it seemed to me a tinge of grey had appeared in his face. The eyes were staring now, focused above my head on the white-haired man.

'Very interesting, Mr Faraday. I would appreciate a little more detail.'

'Nothing much to it,' I said. 'You know what happened at the club. Green's goons jumped me. It was over-reaction to a simple inquiry. Especially as Erika's agent, Leroy, was certain she was on vacation at Lake Arrowhead.'

Roco put his two hands together and cupped them round his right kneecap. He rocked to and fro for a moment or two.

'I might have found out a little more if it hadn't been for your friend,' I said. 'Shortly after that the roof caved in.'

Roco smiled thinly.

'It happens to all of us at times, Mr Faraday,' he said softly. 'But I'm sure you know all about that.'

I nodded.

'I spend most of my time waking up among the trash-cans on back lots," I told him.

'Either you are a very simple man or you are telling the truth, Mr Faraday,' he said.

I shook my head, stopped when I felt the front of my face might fall off.

'Try the latter, Mr Roco.'

He swayed to and fro some more.

'That's what I figured. How do you read the situation?'

'There is no situation, so far as I can see. Maybe Erika has just gone off on her own to sort out some problem. The girl Tina seemed very timid and self-effacing to me. She may be worrying over nothing. My next move was to check the hotels around Arrowhead.'

Roco was still frowning at his nails.

'A very sensible procedure, Mr Faraday. Or you may have come to me in any event?'

2

There was a heavy, thunderous silence in the apartment now that was entirely due to the close atmosphere. The lamps shone on blandly in the warmth and the stillness. I kept my eyes away from the French windows, concentrated on looking beat-up, and awaited my moment.

'That was on the cards too,' I said. 'You were Erika's friend, after all. That was common knowledge.'

Roco abruptly took his hands away from his knees and examined his nails.

'Perfectly true. But what makes you think I'd know where she was? We split up some while ago.'

He fixed the strange-coloured eyes back on my face.

'Where is Tina, Mr Faraday?'

'I thought you knew,' I said. 'The two girls lived in the same apartment. I've never been there.'

Roco gave me a wolfish smile.

'Neither have I. But I know where it is. I'd like to ask her some questions. I'm sure she'd find her sister if she went up to Arrowhead.'

'Sure,' I said. 'Except there's some pieces missing somewhere.'

Roco studied his nails again.

'What makes you think that?' he said slowly. I tried another smile. The effect was better this time.

'Come on, Mr Roco. Even people like Green don't come unglued when a P.I. makes a simple missing persons inquiry. The people at the club had only to mention Lake Arrowhead when the girl phoned. But the heavies at The Blue Parrot started making with the flak. Green went to pieces, like I said. Then you have me outed and brought here by two very smooth pros. All for a little girl like Erika Matthews, who's gone on vacation for a few weeks. It doesn't add up.'

Roco smiled at his nails.

'You're right, Mr Faraday,' he said dreamily. 'There has to be something else.'

He straightened on the back of the chair, looking down at me benignly.

'And you'd have to keep digging, wouldn't you?'

I grinned.

'Maybe.'

'No maybe about it,' Roco said. 'I have your track record, Mr Faraday.'

He traded glances with the man at the door again.

'Waste him,' he said.

I was out the chair before anyone could move. My right shoe came up in a shining arc, caught Roco on the knee. He gave a groan of pain and somersaulted backward over the divan. I had the heavy chair I'd been sitting in now. I ran it straight at the French windows, watching white-hair's shadow out the corner of my eye.

There was the crash of breaking glass which seemed to split my skull apart. The doors held. They were stronger than I figured. I hit them again as Roco went on rolling and groaning. There was an angry twittering noise then and something tore a long strip of wood from the window near my head.

I dropped to the floor as the slug went whining around the room. The next tore a long groove in the plaster and sent choking clouds of dust about the place.

I hefted the chair away from me before white-hair could get a third off. He was halfway across the room when the heavy mahogany and leather piece tore into his legs. There was a dull cracking noise and he turned an abrupt somersault. He and the chair hit the floor with a crash that seemed to rock the building. All this had taken perhaps fifteen seconds.

The silenced pistol fell a yard from me with a thump. I got to it as Roco wriggled away toward the far door. I tore off a strip of wallpaper near his head before he wriggled into the bedroom. I put the last two slugs through the door-lock of the French windows.

I went through like Paavo Nurmi in his heyday. Then I was in the open air, making great time down the lawn. The sedan was parked where I figured it was. I could see its bonnet gleaming in the moonlight. The big wheelman was off guard.

He was running around the wrong side of the bonnet when I hit from the rear, coming off the lawn edge in a tearing dive down on to the gravel. I caught him behind the ear with the silencer and he somersaulted, the big automatic skittering.

He lay where he fell and I had no time for the gun. I was already behind the wheel, reaching for the ignition. The keys were still in. The engine fired first pull and I went down the driveway, taking about six pounds of rubber off each tyre. I went over the ankle of the big man but I couldn't avoid that. It was either him or me.

You're getting real mean, Faraday, I told myself. I flipped off the mainbeam when I got on to the secondary road and drove on sidelights alone. There was enough moon for that. At the first intersection I turned back, away from L.A., looking for another fork.

I was in no state for a pursuit and shoot-out on the hairpins. I didn't know how badly hurt white-hair and the big man were but Roco was certainly uninjured and he hadn't struck me as the sort of character who gave up easily.

I'd have to go to ground for a few days until I found out what the score was. The only thing I regretted was the Smith-Wesson. It had been with me a long time. I turned on to another secondary road that went downhill, guiding myself by the distant lights of L.A. I'd be able to find my way all right now and I knew these boys would never be able to trace me tonight.

They'd figure I'd take the shortest route in. This is where a hunted man always scores over the opposition. He has to be smarter than his opponent because the stakes are higher in his case. I turned the wheel again; I was over-correcting on the curves, unfamiliar with the handling of the big sedan.

I was straightening up when the moonlight through the windshield glinted on something lying on the passenger seat at my side. I reached over, the chill of metal on my finger-tips. I put the Smith-Wesson back in my shoulder holster, felt properly dressed then.

It took me an hour to hit the city and I circled around for a while until I was certain there was no-one outside Alex Leroy's office block. I still had all my money, my wallet and my car-keys, though it was obvious that white-hair had been through my stuff. He wouldn't miss a simple trick like that. Even the girl's picture was still there.

I parked in the deep shadow of a flowering hedge and put the sedan keys down a nearby storm-drain. Then I opened up the bonnet and did as much damage to the wiring as I could without making any undue noise. By the time I got back in the Buick and started heading west I felt I'd done a pretty good evening's work.

CHAPTER NINE

1

It was around ten o'clock when I got to the girl's place. I'd stopped in at a small restaurant on the way over and got outside a steak and some coffee. After that I felt I might live with a little care and kindness. I'd gotten to a payphone and raised Stella. I'd given her a rundown on the situation, without over-emphasising the set-up.

She'd taken notes and hadn't asked too many questions with that marvellous tact of hers. Like me she'd agreed it was essential that I talked to Tina Matthews again. What I couldn't understand was why Roco hadn't approached the girl before. She might be in danger now and I had to warn her too and get her to a place of safety.

I'd asked Stella to ring a woman who ran a small private hotel on the other side of town, which I'd used several times before. The proprietor was discreet and no-one would know we were there provided I stashed the Buick out of sight in one of the lock-up garages.

I'd told Stella I'd be in touch tomorrow and rang off. Now I circled around the block I wanted, looking at the automobiles parked beneath the garish lights of the lamps set atop steel poles around the perimeter of the lot. I couldn't see anything suspicious but I kept on going until I was certain there was nothing out of the way.

Then I drove on a couple of blocks and parked my heap in a dark alley at the rear of a warehouse building. I walked on back down, avoiding the lights from restaurants and other occupied buildings and keeping in the shadow as much as possible. The bulk of the Smith-Wesson made a reassuring pressure against my chest muscles; I'd checked it out and it still held the five slugs and the spare clip I always carried in the harness.

I'd thought some more about Leroy on the way in. Roco's pro had obviously held a gun on him from behind the door. I'd have done exactly the same in his circumstances. And I was convinced that he really believed Erika Matthews was vacationing at Lake Arrowhead. It was true, like I'd told Roco, that I had thought of going up there. But I could waste days checking hotels and in the meantime an organisation like Roco's could easily pick me up again.

My best bet was to remain in the city and keep on pushing. Green would collapse with one more shove. He was the weakest link in Roco's organisation and he'd split right open at my next push. I guessed that he wouldn't know much. But he might just know enough to lead me to Erika or at least an explanation of her disappearance. And possibly the racket that was involved.

That there was a racket I was convinced. I had a nose for such things. White-hair and Roco hadn't been fooling. They would have killed me tonight if I hadn't acted first. I'd caught them off balance once. They wouldn't give me a second chance.

From now on I had to shoot first in order to stay alive. And like always I was walking in the dark. I decided to keep on going. Tina Matthews had come up with some of the folding stuff and I owed it to her to plug on to the end.

I was up opposite the big apartment block now; I'd crossed the boulevard farther down and I cruiscd on, keeping a sharp eye on the parking lot, the trim hedges and the manicured lawns that fronted the place. There was a flag flying at the top of a white-painted pole in the grounds; it had some symbol on it but it was lying limp and flaccid in the wilting breeze so I couldn't read what it was.

I crossed the boulevard again a hundred yards farther down and cased the parked automobiles; none of them had any drivers and it was unlikely anyone would be lying on the floor inside one of them on the thin chance that I might show.

But I left the area and turned at right-angles down the next boulevard. There was a high hedge here which screened me and I found a gap a little way along and got on the grass side, keeping the hedge between me and the street.

There was a dim light burning over a side door to the apartments which I figured might be a service or fire exit. The odds were that there wouldn't be any receptionist or janitor there. It depended on how swanky the apartments were.

I eased up under the lamp without anyone blowing a hole in me and felt beads of sweat trickling down my cheeks. I got inside the big swing door as quickly as I could. It was a service entrance all right. There was nothing in here but a couple of laundry trolleys on rubber tyres; and the hum of the air conditioning.

I knew the number of the girl's apartment and that she lived on the fourth floor. I also had her phone number jotted down somewhere. I looked it up from my notes, a nerve fretting in my cheek. I rounded a turn in the corridor and found a house-phone in a small glassed-in booth.

2

I guessed it was for the janitor's use and as there was nothing ahead of me but the service staircase and no doors leading off I figured it was safe to use it. I went on over and dialled the girl's number, hoping one of the service

77

phones wouldn't ring somewhere else in the building. Nothing happened; I listened to the dialling tone and the steady pumping of my heart.

I stood there for what seemed like hours but must have been all of three minutes. I put the phone back on the cradle in the end and gum-shoed over to the foot of the stairs. I got the Smith-Wesson out the holster and held it in my trouser pocket, just in case I needed it in a hurry.

Like everything about this case the lack of response could mean anything or nothing. The girl could be out; something may have happened to her; or she could be held in her apartment by one of Roco's goons. There had hardly been time for him to get over here in person, even allowing for my short stop at the restaurant, but he had a long arm. I knew that from the obituary reports in the quality newspapers.

I walked on up to the second floor, what was left of my brain heavy with thought; listening to the faint tread of my size nines on the composition flooring. They didn't run to carpets here. I checked the service doors on the way up; they were all unlocked and they all led direct to the apartments whose numbers were indicated on the walls inside the lobbies.

That reinforced my feeling that the stairs were also used as a fire escape; there were extinguishers in racks on the walls I noticed as

I mounted to the fourth. It reminded me of the shindig over at The Blue Parrot. It seemed like a million years ago now. Though I'd only been on the case a day or so. If you could call it a case.

I got up to the door leading out into the corridor of the fourth and ducked as a heavy shadow passed across the glassed-in panel. I had the Smith-Wesson out and up and I listened to the heavy tread of footsteps on the carpeting beyond the wall of the corridor. I was sweating heavily. My nerves were more eroded than I thought.

Presently I heard the whine of the elevator going down. I eased out into the corridor. There was nothing but blank, anonymous-looking walls leading into the far distance. I went on down, listening for any untoward noise, holding the Smith-Wesson at the side of my jacket, checking the door numbers. Number 84 was up the far end, on the right, just where the residents' staircase went up into the shadows above.

I guessed a bulb had been blown or removed here and the maintenance people hadn't got around to fixing it; it was the only black patch in an otherwise fairly well-lit corridor and I gave it a sharp once-over. I didn't see anything and went across to the polished pine door with the chrome fittings.

The first thing I noticed was that it was slightly ajar; then I saw it had been forced because there was splintered woodwork around the lock area. My belly muscles were fluttering as I used the Smith-Wesson barrel to slowly push the door inward. The light was still on and I knew then there wouldn't be anyone around.

I went on in and quietly shut the door behind me, hoping no-one from the management would come, because there was no way of locking it. I found a chair and wedged it under the door handle. It would give me time to get down the outside fire escape if anything happened.

I lit a cigarette and put the spent matchstalk back in the pack. I feathered out blue smoke at the ceiling and looked at the apartment. I'd seen some going overs in my time but this was the best yet. I hoped the girl hadn't been home. Else she might be here still. I walked over into the centre of the floor; it was a combined hall-living room, with the hall area separated by polished wooden uprights.

Professionals had been at work; drawers had been opened and their contents emptied on the floor; pictures removed from the walls; even the cushions had been examined because I could see the imprints of claw-like fingers in their velvet surfaces. Yet there was a method in it.

It had been a methodical, systematic search with no hint of vandalism. Nothing had been smashed or destroyed, just turned over. The only thing broken in the place that I could see was the lock to the entrance door. The whole operation bore the mark of the high-grade professional.

I went through the entire apartment. There were five rooms in all, including the kitchen and bathroom and the scene was the same throughout. Even the lid of the low-level toilet suite had been removed. I went back in the living room, cleared space on the divan and sat down. As I finished my cigarette I went over the possibilities in what remained of my mind.

That the search was connected with the disappearance of Erika Matthews I had no doubt. But what were they looking for. Some clue to her whereabouts? Or something else that was eluding me for the moment. My head was throbbing again nicely now and I soon gave it up.

I looked at my watch. It was a quarter of eleven. Time I was hitting the road. It would be almost twelve before I reached the hotel and I could use a sandwich and a nightcap. All this sapping gave one a thirst. I grinned at my jaded reflection in a gilt rococo minor that was hanging crookedly on the far wall.

I thumbed the lights off, using my handkerchief and got out as quickly as I could. I went back down the corridor, still turning over the tumblers of my mind without the cogs meshing in anything.

I must have been half-asleep to be caught

twice the same day. I brought the Smith-Wesson up as a shadow moved in the darkness of the stairway at my back and a hand grasped my shoulder.

CHAPTER TEN

1

'Mr Faraday!'

The girl's face was white and strained as she eased forward into the corridor light.

'You don't know how worried I've been!'

When I came back down from the sixth floor elevator stop I stared at her in silence for a moment. I put the Smith-Wesson back in the holster.

'You nearly got yourself killed,' I said.

Sure as hell it was a mile from the truth but it was all I could think of and I felt pretty silly for the moment. I drew Tina Matthews back into the shadow again, where neither of us could be seen.

'When did they leave?' I said.

The girl sat down on the stair and I sat next her. She still looked like some prim little secretary though this time she was more agitated than before.

'About an hour ago,' she whispered. 'Two big men in white raincoats. I was too frightened to move. What did they want?'

'They were looking for you,' I said. 'Or at least something that might lead them to Erika.'

'Erika?'

The girl's face, dimly seen in the shadow here, was anxious, her lips trembling.

'Have you found out anything about her?' I shook my head.

'A little. But nothing bad. According to her agent, Leroy, she's vacationing at Lake Arrowhead.'

The Matthews number drew in her breath with a husky little sound in the silence of the staircase.

'But why wouldn't she have contacted me?'

'There's a lot more to it,' I said. 'Those men turning your place over were part of it. If you have any information that might help me now's the time.'

'Not here,' the girl whispered. 'I can't stay here.'

'I agree,' I told her. 'It wouldn't be safe. I'm going to take you to a hotel for tonight. I'm going there myself in any case. Tomorrow we'll sort something out.'

I looked at her closely. I could see a little more detail of her features now.

'How did you avoid them?'

She shook her head.

'Just luck, Mr Faraday. I was coming home this evening. I'd been out for a meal. I had a

83

strange feeling. For some reason I took the elevator to the third and then walked up. I heard a funny sound. I looked around the angle of the corridor and saw these two men trying to break into my apartment. I waited until they'd gone inside and then came up on the stairs here. I knew they wouldn't be able to see me and I guessed they wouldn't come any higher in the building. They were looking either for me or Erika.'

'Even so you took an unjustifiable risk,' I said. 'Those men were dangerous. Just how dangerous you have no idea.'

The girl's voice was trembling now.

'I was terrified, Mr Faraday. I didn't know what to do. I was paralysed. They stayed nearly three quarters of an hour. But they were very quiet. Several of my neighbours passed along the corridor during the time they were there but they heard nothing untoward.'

'They were professionals,' I said. 'They turned the place over real good. But they didn't damage anything.'

The girl put a small, pink-nailed hand on my arm.

'But what were they after, Mr Faraday?'

'I was hoping you'd tell me,' I said.

Tina Matthews shook her head again.

'I have no idea, and that's the truth. Who could be behind it?'

'Roco,' I said. 'I've already seen him tonight.'

The girl's eyes were wide and her fingers tightened on my arm.

'What do you mean?'

'It's too long a story to go into now,' I said. 'We'll wait until we get to the hotel. Then we'll see what's the best course to take. You'll have to lie low for a while. I'm lying low myself come to that.'

The girl got up unsteadily. I got up too and put my hand on her shoulder.

'Will it be safe to go back?' she said.

I grinned.

'As safe as it will ever be. I'll keep watch while you get a case and a few overnight things. But don't try to clear up. It would take hours and we haven't the time.'

The girl bit her lip, standing irresolute for a moment.

'But what about my apartment?'

'You can ring up the janitor from the hotel,' I said. 'Tell him to fix the lock tonight. Otherwise, someone might clear the place out.'

The girl nodded. She seemed more determined now. I waited outside for ten minutes while she got her things. It seemed more like an hour but no-one came back. We got down the service stairs without being seen.

There was nothing and no-one suspicious as we picked up the Buick. Then I jammed my toe down on the accelerator pedal and we got the hell out.

2

My cigarette smoke went up in an unwavering line to the ceiling of the deserted dining room. The girl's face was strained and white as she stared at me over her coffee cup but she was coming back to normality. Rain had started to star the windows of the small hotel and the proprietress, who was noted for her tact as well as her generosity, had quickly rustled up sandwiches and other stuff that lay on the table between us.

We were the only people in here as it was after midnight now and the dining room was closed anyway. I'd gathered there were only a few people staying at the moment so I guessed Mrs Corcoran had been pleased to get the extra bookings.

I'd engaged two adjoining rooms and warned the girl to keep her door locked. She didn't need the warning. She was plenty scared all right. She sat looking at me now with wide eyes behind the tortoise-shell glasses.

'You want to tell me all about it, Mr Faraday?' I shook my head.

'Not yet, Miss Matthews. You have enough worries at the moment. Like I said I have a line on your sister. But it could take some while to check out the hotels in Arrowhead.'

Tina Matthews leaned forward across the table. 'Maybe I could help.'

'In what way?' I said.

The girl put her pink-nailed fingers together primly on the check table-cloth in front of her.

'I'm going to be holed-up here for several days according to you? Right?'

'Right,' I said. 'It's going to be too dangerous for you around town until I get this case cracked.'

'So time will hang heavy unless I have something to do,' she said. 'Supposing I get a list of hotels and ring them round, asking after Erika. Without giving away my location, of course. If I strike lucky I'll let your secretary know.'

'Fine,' I said. 'But be careful with your questions. And don't give your real name.'

The girl's eyes were wide with surprise. She was pretty good at that bit.

'Why ever not?'

'Roco has a long arm,' I said. 'I should know. He tried to chop me up tonight.'

The girl shivered suddenly. She put her hand across the table and rested it on the back of mine. It felt cool and pleasant to the touch.

'I'm sorry I got you into this, Mr Faraday.'

'Don't worry about it,' I said. 'There's something big behind it. Something far more important even than the disappearance of your sister.'

I saw Tina Matthews' eyes cloud over, went on to explain.

'I don't mean in human terms, of course. Nothing's so important, particularly from your viewpoint. I meant there's some big racket going on. The character Green over at The Blue Parrot is in it up to his dandruff. Roco, of course. He seemed surprised that your sister had disappeared. He reckoned he hadn't seen her for some time.'

Tina Matthews bit her lip.

'Did you tell him about me?'

'There was no point in not mentioning you,' I said. 'Roco knew where you both lived. I had to have some reason for wanting to find your sister. If I hadn't told him he would obviously have realised you'd hired me.'

The pressure of her fingers on the back of my hand increased.

'Of course, Mr Faraday. Forgive me.'

'Nothing to forgive,' I said. 'There's no doubt that Roco had your place turned over. But why? Unless Erika had something he wanted. Some-thing valuable. And she's gone to ground because of its importance and is afraid even to contact her own sister.'

Tina Matthews slowly released her fingers from mine and withdrew her hand. She stared at me for long moments.

'But that's crazy, Mr Faraday. If she's up at Lake Arrowhead.'

I shook my head.

'We don't know that. It may be a smokescreen.'

I looked at my watch. It was a quarter of one and I knew Mrs Corcoran was waiting up to clear after us.

'It's getting late. We'll discuss this again at breakfast.'

Tina Matthews stood up abruptly. Once again I was aware of the soft, appealing beauty beneath the demure exterior. She flushed.

'I'm sorry, Mr Faraday. I didn't think. It's been such a confused sort of day.'

'You can say that again,' I told her, remembering my own.

'I'll never forget this,' the girl said. 'You've been so good to me.'

I grinned.

'It's what you're paying me for, Tina.'

She shook her head vehemently.

'I don't think so, Mr Faraday. You've been hurt in some way already, haven't you?'

I shrugged. We started walking back down the dimly lit dining room. The patter of rain at the windows was heavier now.

'A bump on the head,' I said. 'Nothing that a good night's sleep won't cure.'

The girl was silent as we went up the stairs together. Mrs Corcoran, a good-looking blonde widow in her early forties met us on the landing. She came forward to shake hands with both of us, like we hadn't already met.

'I hope everything's all right, Mike,' she said.

'Just great,' I said.

She went on down the stairs with long, vibrant strides. Tina Matthews paused outside her bed-room door.

'What will you be doing tomorrow, Mr Faraday?'

'I'll be at my office earlier on,' I said. 'But I'll see you at breakfast, of course.'

There was alarm on the girl's face again. 'But won't that be dangerous, Mr Faraday? Going to your office?'

'Maybe,' I said. 'But I don't think they'll bother me there in daylight. And I have this.'

I tapped the breast of my jacket.

'See you in the morning,' I said.

Tina Matthews leaned forward and put her face up to mine. It was a hungry, yearning sort of kiss that seemed to burn holes in my socks. She pushed me away and looked into my eyes like she could read all sorts of things there.

'What's that for?' I said. 'The promise of things to come?'

She smiled mysteriously.

'Maybe, Mike. Regard it as a down payment. A small token of my gratitude.'

I smiled too.

'I'll look forward to the next instalment.'

She didn't look demure at all as she stood close to me in the dim light of the landing lamp. She ran a pink tongue around red lips.

'There's plenty more where that came from,' she whispered.

I stood there for what seemed a long time after the key had turned quietly in the lock. I only moved away when I saw the amused features of Valerie Corcoran staring up at me from the hall below.

'You're losing your grip, Mike. I remember the day when you would have followed that up.'

I threw her a smile.

'Maybe you're right. But I have to consider the proprieties of your hotel.'

Her hooting laughter trailed after her all the way back to the kitchen area. I went on in to my bedroom, locked the door. I'd stashed the Buick in Valerie's private garage and the girl and I had registered under false names so there was no way anyone could trace us here.

I went over and drew the thick curtains before putting on the bedside lamp. I undressed quickly and put the Smith-Wesson under my pillow where I could get at it in a hurry. The last thing I remembered before I went out was the urgent patter of the rain at the windows.

CHAPTER ELEVEN

1

Stella's eyes were very blue and very serious as her gold pencil went racing across the paper.

'Should you be here, Mike, under the circumstances?'

I shrugged, leaning back at my broadtop.

'Exactly what Tina Matthews said.'

I closed my eyes against the sun-glare at the blinds. My headache had returned.

'You ought to be in bed,' Stella said.

'Coffee would help,' I told her. 'I feel like I'm suffering from jet-lag; this case is moving so fast.'

Stella smiled. It seemed to lighten up the whole office. Today she wore a simple silk dress with a knee-length skirt that shot my morale to hell and back every time she got up and down. The blue of the dress was the same colour as her eyes. It sounds corny but it was just right, like everything else about her.

She went over to the glassed-in alcove and switched on the percolator. I sat on at the desk, salivating, keeping my eyes closed and thinking how great it would be to find some other method of earning a living. I think that way at least twice on every case. This was the first time on the Matthews' problem but it was only the second day. A bad sign.

Stella came back and sat down in the client's chair. She looked at me quizzically.

'I hope you won't mind this, Mike.'

'Mind what?' I said.

She shook the gold bell of her hair diffidently.

'I rang up Police H.Q. after your call last night. I got hold of Lieutenant McGiver. I didn't go into detail but I told him things could get rough. He said he owed you one.'

I raised my eyebrows.

'So?'

'So this,' she said. 'He agreed to put a couple of men and a patrol car on for the next four or five days. They'll follow you around unobtrusively and lean on anyone who tries anything.'

I looked at her for a long moment.

'That will make me really conspicuous,' I told her.

Stella bit her lip.

'I did it for the best, Mike. They'll try and be as invisible as possible. I hoped you wouldn't mind.'

I shook my head.

'I don't mind, honey,' I said. 'And thanks.'

Stella shifted uneasily on the chair and then got up briskly and went back to the alcove. While she was bringing the cups the phone buzzed. It was a man's voice, harsh and grating.

'Faraday?'

'That's what they call me,' I said.

'I'm Harry Popkiss. You maybe heard of me.' I grinned across at Stella.

'The Hotel King. And millionaire gambler. Right?'

'You read too many popular papers,' he said drily. 'But that will do as a brief bio. I hear you're in trouble.'

'First I heard of it,' I said.

He gave a harsh, barking laugh.

'Don't fool around with me, Faraday. I heard Roco tried to part your hair with a lead comb.'

'You hear good,' I said.

He chuckled again.

'I have my contacts. We may be able to help one another. I have some interest in this business.'

I stared across at Stella as she put my cup down and went back for her own.

'What business,' I said innocently.

'You know what business,' he said. 'Roco owes me a lot of money. He tells me it's gone missing. I thought we might pool our knowledge and resources.'

'Sounds inviting,' I said.

'Better than a hole in the ground,' he growled.

'You have a point there,' I told him. 'What would you suggest?'

'I'd like us to meet straight away. Come and have lunch. The Sheraton-Plaza. You know the location.'

'You think they'll let me in?' I said.

He grinned. Don't ask me how I knew. I could sense it clear across town.

'They'll let you in, Mr Faraday. I own the building. Twelve o'clock sharp.'

'I'll be there,' I told him.

It was half-eleven when I quit the office. I hadn't left the Buick in my usual underground parking lot. I figured it was too deserted and too dangerous at this stage of the game. Instead I'd stashed it in a public parking area about three blocks from the office. I walked on down, the bulk of the Smith-Wesson making a nice easy pressure against my shoulder muscles.

My headache had gone now and there was still a slightly fresh feeling in the air following the rain of the previous night. After I'd been walking for a hundred yards I was conscious of a long, low bonnet cruising at the corner of my eye. My hand was halfway to the Smith-Wesson before I recognised the shield and stencil of the L.A. Police Department on the door panel.

Stella was right. It maybe wasn't such a bad idea after all. I didn't make any sign of recognition to the two grim-faced plain-clothes men in the interior but went on down, keeping my eyes peeled, until I got to the place where I'd left the Buick.

I walked on over the concourse, aware that the prowl car had halted some way back. Usually plain-clothes people use plain-clothes vehicles, if you follow what I mean. Maybe they were just making sure the opposition knew who they were.

I got behind the wheel of the Buick and idled on down toward the entrance to the main stem. I kept a sharp eye in the rear-mirror but I couldn't see anything. Nevertheless I got out the Smith-Wesson and put it down on the passenger seat where I could get at it in a hurry. That was how the case was getting me.

I was just on the apron, waiting to slot into the traffic stream when I saw the snout of the big black sedan drift into my wing mirror. I felt better then. I knew where they were and I was ready for them. Apart from which there was a little assistance in view.

It was beautifully done. I was just moving out, turning left into the traffic and the sedan was edging up to take my place when the car driven by the plain-clothes men cut across its snout. There was a lot of faint shouting as I let in the clutch and accelerated up. An enormous man who must have been almost seven feet and who had cop written all over him got out the patrol car and walked over to the sedan.

He slammed the door, pinning the driver back into his seat. There was a symphony of police sirens then. It was a nice set-up. I wondered if white-hair had been aboard. And if any of the people in the sedan had police records. In which case they could spend a long time downtown before they got bailed out. I'd ring McGiver and thank him before the day was over.

Not that I relaxed any on the way across to

the Sheraton-Plaza. There wasn't likely to be anyone else around and for all that I knew McGiver might well have another wagon on my tail. I was used to having my rear exposed and it was a good feeling to be covered for a change. If you know what I mean.

I didn't see anyone else all the way and I made good time; it still wanted ten minutes of twelve when I tooled into the acreage of the hotel parking lot and killed the motor. The Buick was hidden amid a lot of expensive metal in here and it was unlikely that anyone would spot it even if Roco had a contract out on me.

He must have been a very worried man beneath the façade if my small-time operation was endangering him. But if Popkiss had an interest here, and it seemed that he had, then I'd gained a heavy-duty ally. Popkiss was a man who operated strictly within the law but he had powerful friends. He wouldn't hesitate to lean on Roco and his operations if it suited him.

The Sheraton-Plaza was and is an extremely handsome and expensive pile of masonry, steel, chrome, marble and aluminium that points its radio mast some twenty storeys to the sky in about three acres of landscaped grounds. I'd heard one needed a passport to get in the tradesmen's entrance but that was maybe an exaggeration.

I got out the Buick feeling strictly like a second class citizen, conscious of the faint ache

97

at the back of my skull again and the fact that my shoes were scuffed like always. I walked on over toward the far side of the concourse and up the massive flights of steps that led to the bronze and glass canopy that sheltered the entrance. I felt I was in Von Stroheim's Wedding March before I'd gone a hundred yards.

The Sheraton-Plaza sat and sneered, its wide double doors waiting to ingest me.

CHAPTER TWELVE

1

The lobby, when I got to see it, seemed to be crowded with dollar millionaires. There were plenty of well-heeled ladies about too, if you liked that sort of thing. The commissionaire in front of the doors, who looked like Marshal Timoshenko on his afternoon off, didn't exactly bust a gut to open up for me.

I left him attending to the cash customers and walked on through into a lobby which seemed to be floored in Parian marble with the walls made of dyed mink. I wondered what a character like Popkiss would offer in the way of a fee. It didn't look as though he was short of the folding stuff.

There was a guy hanging around the

horseshoe-shaped reception desk who looked like something out of a thirties fashion magazine. He had black shiny hair and wore a cutaway coat and he had under-manager written all over him. He advanced toward me like he was about to direct me to the trade entrance.

"I didn't know marcel waves were back in again,' I said. There was a flush on each cheek now and he eyed me hesitantly.

'I have an appointment with Harry Popkiss,' I said before he could come back. 'The name's Faraday.'

I showed him my identification. He straightened up, a remarkable transformation taking place.

'Yes, sir! Mr Popkiss is expecting you, sir. Penthouse Suite Number One. I'll take you up myself.'

'Now you're swinging too far the wrong way altogether,' I told him.

He smiled at me hesitantly.

'Not at all, sir. Mr Popkiss' every wish is our command.'

'That must be nice for him,' I said.

The tall young man with the million dollar teeth shrugged, leading the way over to the elevator concourse.

'When a gentleman like Mr Popkiss owns the entire hotel and a lot else besides, he's entitled to service.'

'Guess you're right,' I said.

I followed him into an elevator cage that had PRIVATE in big gold letters over the top of it. We rocketed up to the penthouse floor and I got out in the corridor feeling like I was still suffering from jet-lag. There was a faint smile on the features of the young man with patent-leather hair. I guess he figured he was a point or two ahead of me now.

We went down a corridor which had snow-white wall-to-wall carpeting and a lot of expensive oil paintings in gold frames set along the walls. I didn't need to see the ceiling-mounted TV cameras and the hard-faced uniformed guard in a glass booth set discreetly down a small T-junction in the corridor to realise that this was a very expensive set-up indeed.

Not to mention a fortress operation. The three people living in the other penthouses must also be multi-millionaires. Which made them extremely vulnerable and prime targets in today's terrorist-orientated society. The under-manager licked his lips like he could read my thoughts.

'We have to be extremely careful, Mr Faraday.' He shrugged.

'I'm sure you understand the precautions. Everyone who works on this floor is personally vetted. Visitors have to be escorted by principal members of staff. We have guards; television; even chrome-steel doors and bomb-proof walls.'

He gave me a thin smile.

'What a world, sir.'

I nodded.

'You've no need to draw me a diagram.'

The dark-haired character shrugged again.

'Even the windows up here are made of armoured glass. In case of snipers.'

'I take it the less well-heeled guests have to take their chances,' I said.

The smile was erased from his face as though someone had dragged a sponge across it. He stopped in front of the last door and waited; I could see the small TV camera above the door start scanning, operated by some solenoid-activated remote control. There were no windows in the corridor and the effect was airless and claustrophobic. I decided I didn't want to be a millionaire. Multi or otherwise.

There was a buzzing and a light glowed on a metal panel set next the door. The under-manager spoke into the grille on the panel.

'Mr Faraday has an appointment with Mr Popkiss for twelve o'clock.'

He smiled confidentially at me. A green light suddenly glinted on the panel. The dark man smiled again.

'Everything is in order, sir.'

'I take it this is all designed by Fritz Lang?' I said.

'I have never heard of the gentleman, sir. I think the designer was Mr Arno Rothbek, a well-known Scandinavian architect.'

I gave up then. The chrome-steel door panel, skilfully disguised as teak, rumbled back with an almost inaudible sound and we went on in.

2

'If you'll wait here a moment, sir, I'll just check with Mr Popkiss' secretary.'

I sat down on a white leather chair whose crinkled seat was murder on the rump and looked round the circular reception hall. That too had no windows and the walls had delicate murals on them which followed the curves of the circle.

The hospital-type lighting came from three frosted glass fittings that were flush with the ceiling. It looked like a spare set from Things to Come. If that was the decor for a multi-millionaire I'd make do with my rented place. I re-adjusted the set of the Smith-Wesson and stared at the lush green of the tropical plants that writhed from teak trunking set about the white filed floor.

Either they took the plants out for light and air or maybe the room revolved to catch the light when louvred windows slid back. It was that sort of place. I turned at another faint rumble. A door that looked like an aircraft hatch had opened at the far side of the circle; the sill was about six inches from the floor and the under-manager almost took a dive as he caught his foot it it.

It made my day. I got up and wandered over, deciding that I'd step high when my turn came to negotiate it. There was a tall, slim, English-looking girl with tawny gold hair standing in the doorway looking at me with barely-concealed amusement. She held out a cool brown hand, ignoring the man with the marcel wave.

'I'm Deborah Thomson, Mr Popkiss' secretary,' she said. 'So you're the gang-buster.'

I shook my head.

'Hardly, Miss Thomson. Just say I'm the pill-dodger.'

She raised her eyebrows.

'Anyway, Mr Popkiss is impressed. So am I, come to that.'

'Don't build me up too much,' I said.

'Well, goodbye people,' the under-manager said desperately.

Neither of us took any notice and he disappeared with a rumble of concealed machinery.

'He grows on you,' the girl said.

'You could have fooled me,' I told her.

The smile seemed to linger a long time at the corners of her mouth. It was a while since I'd seen anything so beautiful. Apart from Stella, of course. The girl stood back and indicated the metal shell of the aircraft door.

'You think you can make it all right?'

'You should have warned me,' I said. 'I'd have worn my best truss.'

The girl's shoulders were shaking as we went down the big room where the sun spilled in through long windows, diluted by gauze curtains and enormous rattan-type blinds. Any other time it would have been a striking view of L.A. but I was in no mood for scenery this morning.

'You look after Mr Popkiss' affairs?' I said. The girl looked at me over her shoulder. There was a wary look in her eyes.

'Some of them, Mr Faraday. Mr Popkiss' empire is too vast for one person to follow.'

'It must be nice work,' I said.

She shrugged.

'It has its moments.'

We were up by a vast metal desk now, with the circular leather chair behind it facing into the room. The desk was L-shaped and I could see that the girl sat on the right-hand side of the L, facing inward to where Popkiss would be sitting. When he sat there, of course.

There were a lot of electronic gadgets built into the surface of the desk, both in Popkiss' area and on the girl's side and what looked like a battery of fifteen or sixteen white telephones that marched along the margin of the desk and round to the girl's seat. There were ticker-tapes too and I recognised a word processor among all the electronic junk.

I expected Dr Mabuse to show any minute but he didn't seem to be around today. I guess I was in a Fritz Lang mood for some reason. Maybe because they'd run a retrospective of his films on TV a few weeks before. The girl sat down at her desk and waved me to a comfortable-looking leather lounger in front.

'Please make yourself at home, Mr Faraday. Mr Popkiss will be through in a moment. Can I get you a drink. Or some coffee?'

'Something long and cool would be fine,' I said.

The girl got up with a faint smile and walked with athletic, rangy strides to the far wall. She pressed a button and a section glided away, propelled by almost inaudible machinery. I saw a bar; what looked like hi-fi equipment; a built-in television; and shelf after shelf of leather-bound books. There was even a movie-projector on a metal stand.

Deborah Thomson busied herself with tall glasses and stirring rods. There was the agreeable clinking of ice. She came back presently and put the greenish-coloured liquid in my hand. In the glass, of course. I tried it; it had limes and alcohol and other stuff in. It tasted great.

The girl clinked her own glass against mine. 'Here's to success, Mr Faraday.'

I nodded.

'I'll second that.'

She looked at me warily.

105

'You carry a gun, Mr Faraday?'

'Sometimes,' I said.

I took another sip at the glass and put it down on a small white table at my elbow. White seemed to be Harry Popkiss' favourite colour. If you could call it a colour.

'Are you carrying one today?'

'Sure,' I said.

I tapped my jacket.

'Is it noticeable?'

The girl bit her lip.

'Of course not, Mr Faraday. So Mr Popkiss wasn't exaggerating? This business is really dangerous?'

'You could say that,' I told her modestly. 'Some heavies tried to intercept me on my way over here.'

There was a flash of alarm in the girl's eyes now.

'What are you trying to tell me, Miss Thomson?'

She uncrossed her legs behind the desk and then crossed them the other way. She looked down into the cloudy depths of her glass.

'Nothing, Mr Faraday. I'm just trying to protect Mr Popkiss' interests. He's a public man. A man in a very vulnerable position.'

'I'm sure,' I said. 'You think I'm bringing trouble to him.'

The girl shook her head.

'Just the opposite, Mr Faraday. Mr Popkiss chose you. I know a lot about Roco, you see.

106

I'm Mr Popkiss' confidential secretary. That means I know most of the important things. About his business, that is.'

She smiled briefly.

'No-one knows everything about any other human being. Isn't that true?'

I raised my glass again.

'I see you're a realist.'

'One has to be in this world, Mr Faraday,' she said bleakly.

She took another sip at her glass and put it down again.

'They tell me you're good, Mr Faraday.' 'I try to be,' I said.

'Good enough for Mr Popkiss?'

I stared her down.

'Good enough for anyone,' I said. 'Question is, is Mr Popkiss good enough for me.'

There was rising indignation in the girl's eyes, which she tried to fight down. A third voice broke the silence in the big room.

'I think we'll get along fine, Mr Faraday.'

CHAPTER THIRTEEN

1

The man who stood in the open door looking down the room toward us was an incongruous sight. He was tall and very fat and his large moon face was bisected by a heavy Che Guevera-type mustache. He had thinning black hair which was cut short so that a lot of it stood out in thick bristles all over his head.

He wore a white silk dressing gown over an open-neck shirt and his feet beneath the grey silk trousers moved like castors under the flowing edges of the gown as he wobbled down the room toward us. For a moment I thought Sidney Greenstreet had come back in his role as Count Fosco.

But there the resemblance ended. I had recognised the rough, almost harsh tones of the man on the phone and as he got up close the features resolved themselves into a contradiction. A man whose almost commonplace human envelope concealed a keen, analytical brain that had made him supreme in business and whose will-power made thousands of employees jump at his bidding. So I didn't under-estimate him.

I got up from the chair and he came forward to give me a warm, limp hand to shake.

'On time, Mr Faraday.'

'Pity you weren't,' I said. 'It's twenty after twelve now.'

He grinned, looking at me shrewdly.

'I appreciate it's a put-on, Mr Faraday, but I like your style. My time is more valuable than yours but I take your point. Any inconvenience will be reflected in the size of your cheque.'

I sat down again, ignoring the scandalised

look of the tawny blonde number.

'That's more like it,' I said.

'I think you have it there,' Popkiss said smoothly.

He took the mauve slip of paper from her without looking at it.

'Five thousand dollars for starters. I hope that is satisfactory?'

'More than satisfactory,' I said.

Popkiss went around his desk and sat in his big circular chair, looking as though he were glued to its surface. He moved surprisingly quickly for a fat man.

'What do I have to do for it?' I said.

He chuckled, rubbing his podgy hands together.

'Nothing more than you're doing already, Mr Faraday. Just keep sticking your neck out.'

I smiled at the girl. She was slightly more relaxed now. She had a pen in her hand and was making notes in shorthand on a pad in front of her. I was surprised. I'd figured she'd have been using an electronic keyboard at least.

'That's a fair enough answer,' I told him. 'You seem to know a lot about my affairs.'

He chuckled deep down in his throat.

'I keep tabs, Mr Faraday. I'm very interested in Roco. And you ran up against Roco. I find that interesting too. Anyone who runs up against Roco is a man on my side. It will pay us both to work together.'

I put the cheque Popkiss had given me in my wallet and took another sip at my drink. The situation was growing more bearable by the minute.

'I'll buy it, Mr Popkiss. But you'll have to tell me a lot more than I know now. You said something about Roco owing you money. How much, for example?'

Popkiss' face had grown hard. He looked at me sombrely.

'A quarter of a million dollars, Mr Faraday. And I want it back.'

2

I glanced across at the girl.

'Sounds reasonable,' I said.

'Very reasonable, Mr Faraday,' Popkiss said softly.

He spread his plump hands on the desk in front of him.

'Not that it's a lot of money. But it's the principle of the thing.'

'Oh, sure,' I said. 'We're talking about loose change here.'

Even the girl smiled. The corners of Popkiss' fleshy mouth beneath the thick mustache widened slightly.

'It's all comparative, Mr Faraday. It may seem like a lot of money to you. My hotel chain alone is worth thousands of millions.'

'You sure your operations aren't too rich for my blood,' I said.

Popkiss shrugged.

'I don't think so, Mr Faraday. Some of your blood may be shed in the process.'

'Or all of it,' I told him. 'I've already had a sample of Mr Roco's hospitality.'

The girl shivered slightly and Popkiss looked at her quickly.

'We mustn't get sentimental, Mr Faraday. This is strictly business.'

I grinned.

'I'm not known for my sentimentality, Mr Popkiss. But I take your point. Let's have some facts. Like how you became involved with Roco.'

Popkiss looked at his well-manicured finger nails.

'It's a long story. I haven't got time to go into it all now. I operate many companies. I didn't know much about Roco then. One of my subsidiaries had financial dealings with a business he owned. The situation evolved from that. These things happen.'

'I can imagine,' I said.

Popkiss went on quietly, like he was talking to himself.

'To cut it very crisp, Mr Faraday, Roco is in to me for a quarter of a million, like I just said. I can't get it back. And Roco is a very dangerous man to press. Even someone like me has to tread carefully.'

111

'I'm listening,' I said.

Popkiss stared at his nails again.

'A month or two ago, as a result of polite prodding by my lawyers, he promised to pay me. An arrangement was made for a settlement in cash. Roco's representatives failed to show up with the money. A man called Green telephoned later.'

'I know him,' I said. 'He's a stooge of Roco's. Manages The Blue Parrot.'

Popkiss nodded, his eyes hooded.

'I am aware of that, Mr Faraday. He is a man to whom a child should not entrust a stick of candy. But perhaps such a creature has his uses for a man like Roco.'

He sighed heavily.

'The gist of his message was that the money ear-marked for me, together with an equal amount had gone adrift. Those were his actual words. There was a valise containing half a million dollars in high-value bills.'

He passed a pink tongue across his lower lip.

'That was no concern of mine, of course. Reading between the lines I felt that perhaps a messenger to whom Roco had entrusted this valise had gone into business for himself. I don't know how that strikes you. But after all, you are an expert in such matters.'

I stared at him for a moment, the cogs in my mind meshing sweetly together. I felt like Popkiss was a man who had my missing half of a hundred dollar bill.

'I think you're dead right, Mr Popkiss. I'll put the rest of the story together for you in a moment.' Popkiss nodded gravely.

'That is excellent, Mr Faraday. My hunch has paid off.'

He frowned at Deborah Thomson.

'Roco's attitude is typical. It is his conceit that it was my money which had gone astray, together with his own. Therefore I won't get paid. I am not having that for one moment.'

He put up a pudgy forefinger and rubbed his heavy jowl.

'It seems from where I'm sitting that my only chance of getting this money is to find the person who took it in the first place.'

I cracked another grin.

'It's great reasoning. But won't this be laundered money?'

There was pain in Popkiss' eyes as he stared at me.

'Please, Mr Faraday! I am a businessman. It is of no concern to me where the money came from. All money is tainted when you get right down to it.'

He smiled suddenly.

'It is the use to which it is put that is either good or bad. That quarter million will finance another project and give employment to fifty or a hundred people.'

'Put like that, you have a point,' I said.

'Most certainly, Mr Faraday.'

He smiled again.

'And there could be another quarter million interest. A percentage of which might be yours.'

'Sounds tempting,' I said. 'But won't Roco object?'

Popkiss' eyes were hard now.

'That's why I'm employing you, Mr Faraday. I hear you're a tough man. Even someone like Roco would have to tread carefully with you around. That's why he tried to waste you straight away.'

I looked from him to the girl. She stared at me blankly.

'You want me to put my head on the chopping block. While you're hoping I'll blow Roco away. Preferably after I've turned up the money.'

Popkiss spread his hands wide once more.

'The stakes are high, Mr Faraday. You're in a high risk business. You can't say I haven't been frank with you. And you do know something of where that money might have ended up?'

I nodded slowly.

'I think I know now. A girl called Erika Matthews has gone missing. Her sister employed me to find her. Erika was Roco's girl-friend at one time. She was a singer. She hasn't been around The Blue Parrot for a while.'

Popkiss made a little smacking noise with

his lips. He looked triumphantly at the girl.

'Excellent, Mr Faraday. And he thought you knew where the girl was. Or the money. That's why he set you up. And is looking for the girl himself.'

'And now you're setting me up,' I said.

Popkiss looked hurt. The girl smiled at me.

'Mr Popkiss isn't used to being spoken to like that, Mr Faraday.'

'He'll have to get used to it if he's around me long,' I said.

Popkiss smiled too.

'We'll get along fine, like I said. I hope you have this girl's sister safe.'

'Holed up securely,' I said. 'She's well enough where she is.'

Popkiss nodded with satisfaction.

'And she knows where her sister is?'

I shook my head.

'That's why she hired me. She was worried about Erika's safety. The girl is supposed to be holidaying up at Lake Arrowhead but that's out now. Someone obviously put that around.'

'You think she's dead?'

'Could be,' I said. 'Maybe she died without revealing where she hid the stuff. And assuming your theory's correct.'

Popkiss sighed again.

'It's a difficult one all right, Mr Faraday. I've given you a problem.'

'My life's one whole problem,' I said.

I finished off my drink and the girl got up to

refresh my glass. I let her do it. Popkiss looked at me bleakly while we waited for her to come back.

'If Roco got to her then he has the money back.'

I shook my head.

'He wanted information from me. And an hour or two later his goons turned over the sister's apartment. We know what they were looking for now.'

Popkiss stared at me for a long moment without saying anything. He waited until the girl had come back with the fresh drinks before he spoke.

'You may be sure of all the backing my organisation can give you in this job, Mr Faraday. And spending money is unlimited. Like I said, it's the principle.'

I looked at him shrewdly.

'You have something else on your mind?'

He licked his fleshy lips again, glancing across to see that the Thomson number was still taking notes.

'I'm just an amateur where your line of work is concerned, Mr Faraday. But something just occurred to me.'

'Shoot,' I said.

'It's just this. Suppose the missing girl left something with her sister. Something in the apartment, apparently innocuous. Without the sister knowing.'

'Something that told where the money was

116

stashed,' I said.

Popkiss' eyes were glinting.

'It's worth a try, Mr Faraday.'

'You're certainly right,' I said. 'I'll drink to that.'

Popkiss got up suddenly, raising his own glass. He gave one of his short, barking laughs.

'You can say that again, Mr Faraday. We'll talk some more about it over lunch.'

CHAPTER FOURTEEN

1

'Popkiss has got his head screwed on right, Mike,' Stella said.

'And then some,' I told her.

It was after four now and I'd just come in. I was still having trouble with the wine and the richness of the Sheraton-Plaza lunch. The place had certainly lived up to its reputation.

Stella went over to the alcove and came back with the coffee. I could use it right now to dilute the wine fumes. Jet-lag wasn't in it this afternoon.

'So my call to McGiver paid off,' Stella said innocently.

'You could say so,' I told her.

She went over to the window, peered down through the blinds.

117

'They're still outside, Mike. Parked up against a fire-plug.'

I grinned.

'Ring downtown and get them booked,' I said.

Stella came back and stood looking down at me.

'Aren't you ever serious?'

'Sometimes,' I admitted. 'You should know.'

Stella flushed and sat down in the client's chair. She slid her cup over toward her.

'No news from the girl?' I said.

Stella shook her head.

'She's sitting tight, like you told her.'

'I hope so,' I said.

Stella wrinkled up her forehead, added a mite more sugar to her coffee. I sat staring at the sunlight making little whorls in the surface of mine.

'Are you going over Tina Matthews' apartment again, Mike?'

'It's a big order,' I said. 'We'll meet tonight and discuss things. She may have some ideas.'

Stella stared at me with very clear eyes.

'You think Erika's dead, don't you?'

I studied the cracks in the ceiling.

'I don't know what to think,' I said. 'Roco and his people wouldn't have killed her unless they'd got the information she may have had. Otherwise why would they be turning over her apartment?'

I switched my gaze to Stella.

'So she may still be holed up somewhere,' she said.

I took another sip at my coffee.

'In which case we're back at first base.' 'It's a heavy case,' Stella said.

'It hadn't escaped me, honey.'

'You didn't show Popkiss the girl's picture?' she said.

I shook my head.

'No point. He'd never met her and wouldn't have known her anyway.'

I looked at her sharply.

'You think Popkiss knows more than he's telling.'

Stella frowned. It didn't affect her beauty any.

'It doesn't seem likely. Possibly he's more worried in case his deals with Roco become public knowledge. It wouldn't help his hotel chain any. That's probably what Roco is depending on.'

'Just keep the stuff coming,' I said. 'You're in good form this afternoon.'

'I'm always in good form,' Stella said. 'And by the stuff I presume you mean coffee.'

'That too,' I said.

I drained mine quickly and watched her fine style all the way across to the alcove.

It was dark by the time I got out to the hotel. The patrol car had kept pace with me for a while and I'd noticed another take over at the edge of town. After that there was nothing and nobody suspicious. I gathered McGiver's people had warned the opposition off in a polite way. Not that that would stop them. But it might cramp their style for a while.

I put the heap away in the private garage and walked back along the rambling façade, enjoying the perfume of tropical flowers and the scent of freshly-cut grass. The sprinklers had been working overtime and the aroma was coming through a treat. I remembered then that Mrs Corcoran was keen on gardening.

There was a blaze of light from the dining room and the bars tonight and half a dozen automobiles out front. I checked them over carefully, noting the details on the licence particulars strapped round the steering posts. There was no-one there who shouldn't be, it seemed to me.

Valerie Corcoran met me in the shadowy hall with its banked masses of cut flowers. She had a warm and open smile.

'How's the girl?' I said.

'Fine, Mike. She's been on the phone most of the afternoon. I guess she's finding Pine Bluffs a little restricting.'

I grinned. Pine Bluffs was the name of the

hotel.

'I don't see why,' I said. 'I find it pretty stimulating myself.'

Mrs Corcoran had a very good figure and she took my meaning. She flushed slightly beneath the tan and shifted her high heels on the tiled paving.

'Maybe, Mike, but you're a man. And don't give me any butch jokes.'

'I won't,' I promised her. 'And let me have the tab for the phone calls. I got an open-ended account on this case.'

She raised her eyebrows.

'My, things are improving.'

'Not before time,' I said. 'Where is Miss Gray?' That was the name I'd chosen for her.

'Up in her room. You're dining in tonight, I take it.'

I put my hand on her arm.

'Where else. And we'll spend an hour or two in a quiet corner of the bar beforehand.'

Valerie Corcoran returned the pressure of my fingers with her disengaged hand.

'Spend away,' she said cheerily.

I watched her progress across the hall as she clattered off to the kitchen regions in rear. There's a fine woman going to waste, Mike, I told myself. Not to mention a first-rate, thriving business. Not that I was into catering myself. But I'm into girls all right. If you know what I mean. And at thirty-three I was beginning to get fascinated with lovely ladies in their early forties.

I pulled my thoughts back to business. I went up to my room and ran a tap over my head. After I'd washed up and made myself more presentable, I changed my shirt and tie and got ready to go down. Stella had been over to my rented house and picked up some things for me, and Mrs Corcoran was providing anything extra the girl needed.

It was around eight when I went along to her room. There was no answer to my knocking at first and I had to repeat it before a low, subdued voice answered.

'Faraday,' I said. 'We should have agreed a code.'

She opened the door at once.

'Mike! It's good to see you. I've never known the time drag so much.'

She looked great. Tonight she wore a plain white sweater that hugged her figure and a grey skirt cut on classical lines that set off her long legs beautifully. She seemed to gleam and coruscate with health and wholesomeness from tip to toe. But with an underlying sexuality that gave her an edge over girls with more obvious charms.

Maybe it was something to do with the tortoise-shell glasses and the way the light shimmered on them.

'Come on in. I was just finishing my nails.'

I followed her into the room, locking the door behind me. I sat on a basket chair at the head of the bed while she went to sit on the coverlet. She picked up the small brush she'd put on a sheet of newspaper and started skilfully applying the pink varnish.

'How was your day?' I said.

She shook her head, concentrating on the nail job.

'Boring. The hours seemed to drag.'

'You had no luck with Lake Arrowhead?'

'I must have tried at least fifteen hotels. The difficulty was getting the numbers. I couldn't get hold of an accommodation list and I had to go through the book picking out hotels at random.'

'I know the drill,' I said, remembering all the times I'd done the same thing.

She stopped what she was doing and raised her eyes. For some reason then she reminded me of Popkiss' secretary, the Thomson girl. I was certainly getting a selection of lovely ladies on this case; not that I was getting very close to them. Unless one excepted the incident outside Tina's room door last night.

'What do you think happened to Erika, Mike? Something really bad?'

'Bad enough,' I said. 'I have another client on the same case now. He seems to think someone made off with Roco's pay-roll. I hate to say it but it may be your sister was involved.'

I saw the rising anger in the girl's eyes and went on before she could interrupt.

'I'm keeping an open mind, of course, but it

123

gives a motive for those goons taking your place apart. Roco was very interested in finding out what I knew before he turned me over to his execution squad.'

The girl bit her lip, making a little convulsive movement with her unoccupied hand against the counterpane.

'You surely can't believe that, Mike.'

'That's what I want to talk about tonight, Tina,' I said. 'You'll have to keep personal feelings out of this as much as possible. These boys are playing for keeps. If they catch up with us it won't be pleasant. And they'll want to put the heat on you. They probably think you know where the money is.'

The girl looked bewildered and lost now. I went over and sat next to her on the bed, put my arm round her shoulder.

'We have to talk, honey,' I said gently. 'Maybe you'll remember something that will help.'

She turned up her eyes and held mine for a long moment.

'I want to clear this up as much as you do, Mike.'

I nodded.

'It might not be too difficult if we know what direction to take. And I have a millionaire's muscle and man-power behind me now. For what it's worth. But it might help to keep Roco off our necks.'

The girl suddenly seemed to crumple. She

came into my arms and sat there passively, the perfume of her hair fragrant in my nostrils. We sat there for what seemed like a long time. Then she raised her mouth and kissed me gently.

'You're a remarkable man, Mike Faraday,' she whispered. 'I feel safe with you.'

I put her gently away and stood up.

'I feel safe with myself, sometimes,' I said. 'This isn't one of them. We'd better go on down and grab that drink before dinner.'

The girl smiled and got up too, putting the last touch to her nails.

'I suppose it's too much to ask you to tell me everything you've learned so far.'

I looked at her seriously.

'It's safer for you not to know at this stage,' I said. 'If your sister has made off with this money and I find out where, that's one thing. If you know everything I do and Roco catches up with you, that's a different matter.'

The girl shivered again and put her hand on my arm.

'I see what you mean, Mike. But it's hard. I love my sister.'

'Sure you do, Tina,' I said. 'But it's the only sensible way. You hired me to find your sister, not to run your neck into a noose. I'll tell you everything I possibly can.'

We walked slowly over toward the door together.

'Even if it's bad,' she said.

I nodded.

'Even if it's bad.'

She held her eyes with my own as I opened the door, made sure the corridor was clear.

'You don't think she's dead?'

I kept my voice non-committal.

'They wouldn't still be looking for her or what she carried if they'd already caught up with her.'

'That's something to be thankful for.'

Tina Matthews put her arm in mine as we went quickly down the stairs together.

CHAPTER FIFTEEN

1

The tinkle of a blues number impeccably played on a grand piano drifted across the bar from the hi-fi system, the wet blue and green notes seeming to disperse my cigarette smoke that was hovering around the ceiling. There were quite a lot of people in, most of them sitting up at the bar; but this booth was in a quiet, shadowy corner.

Mrs Corcoran had made sure of that by putting a reserved sign on it. We were on our second glasses of white wine before Tina Matthews thawed out. Since we'd been in here she'd appeared listless and preoccupied but now that the small talk was over she was more animated.

'You spoke earlier of ways that I could help. What ways?'

I looked toward the blonde head of Mrs Corcoran near the bar, as she bent forward to listen to the same sort of slurred chit-chat that she must have heard most every evening of her life in the hotel business. It was one thing that would have bored the mind out of me within a few weeks.

'There are a number of ways, Tina. I want to know everything you can tell me about Erika. Where she went and with whom. What she said the last week she was with you; what her preoccupations were.'

I lowered my voice as a couple drifted past. I gave them a sharp onceover as they sat down opposite. They were out of earshot anyway but I still didn't raise my tones.

'Above all I want to know if she left any instructions or messages for you, however trivial, that would give me a lead.'

The girl put down her glass of wine deliberately. She looked vaguely round the room, lingering in turn on each of the people present.

'You want chapter and verse, Mike?'

I nodded.

'We have the time. That's what we're here for.'

I picked up a yesterday's newspaper that

someone had left on one of the banquettes in the booth and put it down by my side. I jotted a few notes unobtrusively on the margin of the paper as the girl talked on about her sister and their life together. She was hesitant, but thorough and as she gained confidence a fragmentary picture began to emerge; of a talented but wayward and headstrong personality who had gotten mixed up with Roco and then regretted the relationship.

The girl kept her head down toward the table, occasionally sipping her wine, and then returning to her monologue in a low, well-modulated voice with clearly enunciated syllables. I don't know why all this stuck in my mind so clearly through my hurried note-taking but it seemed to me once or twice as though she were reciting something long rehearsed.

For one crazy moment I figured it might have been information Erika had told her to repeat before she disappeared but then I dismissed the possibility. There was no doubt the girl was sincere; she was genuinely distressed at her sister's disappearance; and she had no more idea where she was at the present moment than I had.

She finished at last and I totted up my notes. They didn't amount to much. But then I hadn't expected them to. She shook her head, looking at me anxiously.

'I haven't been much help, have I?'

'Don't worry,' I said. 'No-one expected this to be easy.'

I watched Mrs Corcoran striding down the room toward us.

'We'll take this up again later.'

Valerie Corcoran came to a halt, looking from me to the girl with amused interest.

'Dinner's ready, Mike. You'd better come on in and get it while it's there.'

2

It was past ten before we had another chance to talk privately. Dinner had been excellent but the tables had been rather close together and we'd had to indulge in trivia. The girl was more outgoing and it was obvious that the intimacy and privacy of this small hotel had given her a feeling of security.

It had just the opposite effect on me and I was never unaware of the presence of the Smith-Wesson in its harness beneath my lightweight jacket.

It wasn't that I expected white-hair to actually show up in the entrance to the dining room but it was no bad attitude in our situation; and it kept my reflexes greased when others around us were merely well-oiled.

We went back into the bar for a night-cap. It was half-empty now though there were a few people who had just come for dinner and who weren't staying in the hotel. I'd had that from Valerie Corcoran herself. She'd stopped by the table once or twice to make sure we were being looked after.

The girl seemed uneasy again. We sat up at the bar this time and she kept staring around her like she was expecting someone to show. She was putting me off balance and I shifted around so that I could see the entrance to the bar.

Tina waited until the dark-haired girl who dispensed the drinks had moved away.

'Mike, there is something I must tell you. I don't know how to begin.'

I smiled at her over the rim of the glass.

'It isn't very difficult, Tina. Just open your mouth and let the words come out.'

She shook her head.

'I'm serious, Mike.'

Another party of people had drifted out the dining room. Four of them sat down next us.

'It's not private enough,' I said. 'Save it until we get upstairs again.'

She gave me a strained smile.

'I may not be in the mood then.'

Before I could reply there came another group of people through the doors, who sat down the other side. We finished our drinks and went back out in the hall. We stopped near the foot of the staircase as though by mutual consent. We couldn't be seen from outside because the hall went round at an angle here.

'There was one thing we didn't get on to properly before dinner,' I said. 'I asked you if there was any message Erika had for you the week before she disappeared.'

Tina Matthews was hesitant again.

'I don't think there was anything, Mike. We partly covered it.'

'That's not good enough,' I said. 'I want to be absolutely sure. It doesn't matter what it is. Anything, however trivial or routine.'

We were walking slowly up the stairs together, the girl keeping in close to the wall like its massive bulk was giving her reassurance.

We got to the door of her room and I waited while she unlocked it. We went on in and I snubbed the catch to behind us. The room looked as bleak and cheerless as only a hotel room can look, though it was pleasant enough. The girl put her key down on a coffee table in the centre of the room and I went to sit in the basket chair.

'You sure there's nothing? She didn't give you anything? A package, maybe?'

There was something hammering at the back of my mind about the Matthews case. There had to be an answer staring me in the face. Roco was looking for something important. And Popkiss was convinced it was half a million dollars. The girl couldn't simply have disappeared. Either she had been killed. Or was hiding out. Either way she would have made sure of a safe place for the money. And she wouldn't have left anything on her which might lead to where she'd stashed it.

Tina Matthews had been thinking, her brow barred with concentration.

'There was something, Mike,' she said with a nervous little laugh. 'It's my birthday next week. Erika gave me a present and told me to take care of it just in case she was out of town. I didn't think anything of it at the time. She made a joke of it and said I wasn't to open it until the due date. But she hoped to be with me, of course.'

I felt a faint stirring of the hairs on the nape of my neck. It's an infallible sign with me. My voice was a little unsteady when I spoke.

'You wouldn't have it with you by any chance?'

'Sure, Mike. I always keep it by me. It's only a small package and I figured it might be jewellery or something valuable. So I put it in my bag. I have it right here.'

CHAPTER SIXTEEN

1

There seemed to be an oppressive silence descending on the room when the girl finished speaking. A weight was on my chest and I could hardly breathe. The girl picked up the brown paper package from a compartment in her bag. She nervously tore off the folded card that was taped to it.

'A personal message, Mike,' she said apologetically.

'Sure,' I said. 'But I think we're going to have to open that package, despite what your sister said. Would you do it now, please.'

There was puzzlement in Tina Matthews' eyes.

'Certainly, Mike. If you think it's important.'

'It's important,' I said.

The sound of ripping paper seemed to split the room apart. The girl was breathing heavily, obviously infected by my manner and I felt a faint vibration in the tips of my fingers as she opened up the package. The brown paper fell aside to reveal a small cardboard box.

There was a separate enclosure, folded in tissue paper, which was taped to the box itself. Tina Matthews opened it, her eyes sparkling. She held up the beautifully crafted set of gold earrings.

'Aren't they beautiful, Mike.'

'Sure,' I said. 'But they're not exactly in the forefront of my mind at the moment.'

I tapped the cardboard box with my forefinger.

'I'd like to see what's in that if you don't mind.'

The girl shook her head, reluctantly putting

down the earrings on the bedside table. She opened up the box and stared at its contents. It was a very expensive toilet set, made by one of the best French perfume manufacturers. I tried not to let the disappointment show on my face. If I didn't strike gold here then I never would on this case.

The girl had already struck gold, of course, but that was a different matter. I had something far more serious on my mind. I took the box from her, stared at the tiny bottle of perfume; the miniature container of talcum powder; and the delicately perfumed cake of soap.

Wheels were slowly turning in the back of my mind. They were rusty, but they were turning. 'I'd like to check these out.'

'Surely, Mike.'

I removed the contents and went carefully through the box. The girl watched me intently, as I probed and pushed, trying to see if something had been taped to the cardboard interior. There was nothing.

'If you'd let me know what's on your mind, Mike, maybe I could help.'

I shook my head.

'It was just a hunch, Tina.'

I took the cake of soap from her, hefted it in my hand. It felt a little heavier than it should have done. I had one of my flashes of brilliance then. I get them about once every thirty years.

I took the soap over to the overhead room light, held it up. I could see the faint outline of something solid in the centre.

'What is it, Mike?'

The girl was at my side, her forehead puckered with curiosity.

'It may be the jackpot,' I said. 'But it means spoiling this.'

'Go ahead and spoil it.'

I went over to the wash-basin at the far end of the room and switched on the mirror light. I broke up the tablet under the running water. Something clattered its way to the bottom of the basin. I'd already sealed it with the rubber plug. I probed thoughtfully at the accumulated soap. I could feel a tingling sensation that went clear from the crown of my head down to my shoes.

Usually such a powerful arousal was only triggered by the presence of a beautiful woman. So if I got the same reaction from a cake of soap it had to be the answer to my problems. I cleared the last of the lather from the metal object and dried it with a towel.

I held out the silver-coloured key in the palm of my hand so the girl could see it clearly. The metal tag attached to the handle by a metal ring bore the number 509.

'This mean anything to you?'

The girl shook her head.

'Should it?'

'It's got to be important,' I said. 'It's the key

135

to a locker. Maybe where your sister stashed the money.'

I ignored the hurt look in Tina Matthews' eyes.

'The question is, where?'

The girl's lower lip was trembling.

'I don't see this will get us any farther forward.'

'Maybe not,' I said. 'But there can't be many places with that number of lockers.'

I kept on staring at the key in my hand like it held the answer to everything about the Erika Matthews case. It most probably did. But I knew it all depended on how I used it.

'But why would Erika put that in my gift? It doesn't make sense, Mike.'

I disagreed.

'It makes all the sense in the world. The earrings were your real present. This gift box was a phoney. She knew you probably wouldn't use it for months. So she could reclaim it.'

'I still don't understand, Mike.'

I shrugged.

'All she had to do was buy an identical set and switch them over after you'd opened your birthday package. It's beautifully simple. Maybe she hoped all the fuss would have died down by then and that she'd be beyond suspicion.'

There was anger again in Tina Matthews' eyes.

'You can't prove any of this, Mike. It's all

136

supposition.'

'Certainly,' I said. 'But it's the only thing that fits. Unless you have any better ideas.'

The girl looked at me helplessly.

'You must understand my feelings, Mike. She is my sister. But I'm entirely in your hands.'

2

I put the key down on the table and went to sit next to her. The key gave off little silver flames beneath the soft light of the room lamp. The numbers stared back mockingly.

'What about that key, Mike?'

'I'm thinking on it,' I said.

'A bus station locker, perhaps.'

'Hardly. They don't run to that number. There can't be that many places in the L.A. area.'

Something clicked into position then. I was maybe getting senile. I was smiling as I stared at the girl.

'You just triggered the brain cells, Tina. L.A. International is the most likely place. They must ave thousands of lockers there for left luggage.'

The girl looked at me dubiously, the light gleaming off her tortoise-shell spectacles.

'But it may not be the place, Mike.'

'That's true,' I said. 'But we're no worse off

than we were before. There's no bus, train station or hotel that would have that number. And if this key fits we're in business.'

'What about the other city airports?'

'Too small for this,' I said.

I looked at my watch. It was just coming up to eleven. I went across to the bedside phone and dialled Stella's home number. She came on straight away.

'Mike,' I said. 'I think we got something.'

I filled her in briefly with my reasoning. The girl sat on the edge of the bed and watched me with those demure eyes.

'You want me to take notes, Mike?' Stella said.

'No time,' I said. 'Besides, it doesn't call for a lot of explanation. I've got this locker key. Number 509. That suggest anything to you?'

'There are few places I know of around the L.A. basin that have such numbers, Mike,' Stella said. 'How about L.A. International.'

'Good girl,' I said. 'Just my reasoning but I thought I'd go direct to the master computer.'

Stella smiled. I didn't have to see it but I could feel its warmth coming over the wire.

'So you're going there now. Be careful, Mike.'

'Sure,' I said. 'You know me.'

'You're not taking the girl?' Stella said.

I shook my head.

'It wouldn't be a good scene.'

Tina Matthews had got up now. She came

over to where I was standing.

'I'm not staying here, Mike. I want to know about Erika. And I can't find out by sitting here all night worrying my heart out.'

'She makes good sense,' Stella said.

I hadn't cupped the mouthpiece and she'd obviously heard the relevant dialogue. I looked at Tina Matthews dubiously. Her mouth was set in a firm line.

'We ought to have some insurance in that case,' I said. 'I'm not against it in principle. And I can see how Tina feels.'

'You want me to contact the police?' Stella said.

'Not yet,' I told her. 'I made certain promises to Popkiss, remember. We got two steamrollers here. I don't aim to be crushed between them.'

I grinned at the girl.

'It would be the first time I've been shot by a client.'

Tina Matthews shivered but Stella gave a low gurgling laugh.

'It's been a monotonous case so far, Mike. You haven't had one corpse yet.'

I looked across at an indifferent Victorian oil painting that was hanging on the far wall.

'I wouldn't call it exactly monotonous, honey. But I get your point. And I don't aim to be the first.'

'So you want me to call Popkiss,' Stella said.

'If you can get hold of him,' I told her. 'Tell

him where I've gone and that I may be close to his money. He wants his cash back. So no police yet. He had my word on it.'

'Right,' Stella said. 'What if I can't raise him?'

'Ask the people at the Sheraton-Plaza who his second-in-command is,' I said. 'He'll know what to do. But be discreet about the money and make sure of the status of the person first. We don't want any slip-ups. Roco's people may be still around.'

'You're leaving now?' Stella said.

I looked at my watch again.

'And you're taking the girl with you?'

Tina Matthews was standing close to me. I stared at the stubborn set of her chin.

'It looks like it,' I said. 'She has the expression of a lady who refuses to be left behind.'

Tina Matthews smiled. She seemed very much like her sister's photograph at that moment.

'You can say that again, Mike.'

'That's it, then,' I told Stella. 'Unless you have any better ideas.'

'You seem to be doing pretty well at the moment for an amateur, Mike,' Stella said drily. 'But remember what I said.'

'I'll watch out,' I promised.

I put down the phone and turned to the girl. I broke out the Smith-Wesson and checked the shells, put the spare clip in my jacket pocket. I put the key in my trouser pocket. I stared at the opened package and its contents on the table.

'You'd better put that stuff in a safe place, preferably under lock and key. Just in case someone traces us here.'

The girl came across and put her face against my cheek. If felt warm and good.

'How soon can you be ready?' I said.

Tina Matthews was already going back across toward the dressing table with the stuff.

'Give me three minutes,' she said.

CHAPTER SEVENTEEN

1

It was raining again now and the neons made a blurred dazzle of the sidewalks and road surfaces. The traffic was thinning out and I made good time, despite the conditions. The girl was silent at my side, biting her lip occasionally so I guessed she was still under some tension.

It was natural enough. She didn't want to believe her sister was a thief who had decamped with half a million dollars of the organisation's money. I could understand that. But there was something else. Something that concerned the two of us; something more subtle that was eating at the edges of her nerves and eroding the rapport that had been built up between us over the last few days.

The neon dazzle through the windows made a shimmering mass of her hair and the whiteness of her teeth was accentuated beneath the redness of the lips. I glanced across at her, forcing her to lift her eyes to mine.

'You're along on one condition, Tina.'

'And what's that, Mike?'

I turned off the side-road on to the main-stem and waited for the lights to change. The signs across the highway were giving the turn-off for L.A. International now.

'You know well enough,' I said. 'This could be dangerous. Roco's a man who doesn't give up easily.'

The girl reached out in the semi-darkness of the car and put her fingers hesitantly on my arm.

'What do you want me to do, Mike?'

'Nothing,' I said. 'Leastways, nothing without my permission. Keep close to me and do exactly as you're told. Understand?'

She nodded. Her face looked white and strained in the rear-mirror. I was keeping a sharp eye on it too. I hadn't seen any signs of anyone following us. But if they were pros they'd be hard to spot; and they'd probably switch vehicles.

I hadn't seen any sign of McGiver's boys,

come to that. Though he may have withdrawn them by now. There was only so much public money the Department could afford to waste in giving protection to someone like me. The brilliantly-lit overhead signs were coming up now, straddling the highway, indicating the lanes for L.A. International.

I signalled and changed over, watching the traffic in my rear-mirror. Nothing happened on this occasion. I wasn't thinking about Roco or McGiver for the moment. The way most Angelenos drive it was unusual enough to be recorded somewhere. The girl remained silent as the Buick bored on.

I guessed she had a good deal on her mind but she'd unburden herself at the right time. I could hear the scream of jet engines accelerating clear above the traffic; and the lights of the terminal buildings were coming up. I signalled off again and queued in the slipway to one of the entrance gates to the parking areas.

I lit a cigarette, feeling the pressure of the Smith-Wesson and the coolness of the locker key against my leg through the lining of my trouser pocket.

We moved on slowly, bumper to bumper, watching the restless scene under the floods, absorbing but not really registering the navigation lights of aircraft against the velvet backdrop as they took off and landed. It took us almost twenty minutes to park the heap.

2

The girl kept close to me as we threaded our way through the concourse. Lights glared down and the rumble of trolleys, the buzz of voices, the clatter of feet and the crackle of the loud-speaker system added to the pleasure. There were so many thousands of people in here it was impossible to keep tabs on any of them.

After three minutes I didn't bother. I'd been involved in a shoot-out here once and it hadn't been pleasant. I'd meet trouble when it came but not before. To that end I'd transferred the Smith-Wesson to my trouser pocket and kept my hand on the butt as we filtered through the crowds.

I knew there was an Airport Police Office somewhere near the locker area if I remembered correctly; if anything happened I'd try to get the girl out and then run like hell.

'Weren't you trying to tell me something earlier?' I said. 'When we were at the bar?'

There was so much noise in here I had to repeat the question. The girl shook her head, her lips set stubbornly again.

'The moment passed, Mike. I'll get to it in due time.'

I looked at her closely.

'And the moment isn't now?'

She smiled faintly, shaking her head.

'That's right. I'm just wondering what you

144

might think of me.'

I smiled back.

'I think you're pretty good, if you want the truth.'

The shadow had returned to Tina Matthews' face.

'You don't understand, Mike. There was something I wanted to tell. I've got to get straight with you.'

'There'll be plenty of time,' I said.

I looked at her bowed profile as we went round a magazine kiosk. The mass of people was so thick in this corner it was like being caught in a mill-race.

'As long as it's not really bad.'

She smiled faintly again.

'Not really bad, Mike.'

'That's all right, then,' I said.

The girl averted her glance.

'It still makes me feel ashamed.'

I put my hand on her arm and steered her away from the crowd. A luggage trolley whirled by, suitcases and hand baggage dancing on its train of rubber-tyred trailers. We were over in the luggage area now. It was quieter in here, the noise of the airport muffled by the long rows of steel lockers that seemed to stretch to the horizon.

There were numbers on boards hanging from the ceiling which gave the disposition of the aisles. We'd walked some way already and had got only to 190. The girl held my hand now, like a child out for a walk with its father. She put her mouth up close to my ear as we went on down the long gangway, our footsteps giving back echoes like we were in a cathedral.

'Do you really expect to find all that money in the locker, Mike?'

I shrugged.

'If not in here then at least in some locker somewhere else. Maybe in another airport.'

The girl's voice was so low I had to strain to listen.

'Assuming my sister is involved in all this, the locker could be in Chicago or New York.'

We had stopped at the angle where two aisles intersected. There were a number of people around in here, depositing and retrieving luggage and I wanted to give them the onceover before we went on.

'It doesn't ring true. Firstly, she left the key in L.A. Your sister gave you that package and wrote you that card. The key was in the cake of soap.'

The girl had a blank, shuttered look now and didn't reply.

'Besides, she didn't have time to get to New York or Chicago according to you,' I told her. 'She was going to The Blue Parrot every night like usual. And she handed you that package for your birthday the night before she disappeared.'

'That's true.'

The voice was still low and faint.

'So that brings us back to L.A.,' I went on. 'Even assuming she could have flown out for a few hours she'd still have all that inconvenience when she retrieved it.'

The girl looked at me with sharp eyes.

'So she must be close to L.A. somewhere.'

'That's what I figured,' I said. 'Which made the Lake Arrowhead location sound so plausible."

We went on down past the next aisle. I kept on checking off the numbers. We were up over 300 now. My legs would be worn down to stumps if this kept up. There were still few people about in here, none at all in the next aisle. I didn't like the location but there was no choice if we wanted to finish the case.

Not that it was ever likely to be finished the way I was going. Even if I came up with the money we still didn't know what had happened to Erika. Assuming she was dead I had to nail Roco for the killing. Or somebody. The more I turned it over in what was left of my mind the greater the number of holes I was finding.

Like always the solution was probably relatively simple; assuming one had all the pieces. I gave up beating my brains out and concentrated on this evening. The girl was evidently turning things over herself.

'Supposing that key doesn't fit, Mike?'

I gave her a twisted grin.

'Then we're back at the starting line again.'

I squeezed her arm gently.

'Let's just take one problem at a time.'

The next aisle slid by. The four hundreds were coming up now. It couldn't be much farther. I turned down the first right, kept on going. We were still short of our destination but I thought it might be better to approach it obliquely. We were hidden by the massed ranks of the lockers in here and it would make it more difficult to pick us out if anyone were watching.

It was true I hadn't seen anyone. But that didn't prove anything. Traditionally, the shell that hits you you never hear coming. Or some such aphorism of von Moltke, if I remembered my modern history.

I snapped my mind back to the present, the Smith-Wesson butt warm and comforting against my fingers as we turned to the left at the end of this enormously long alley and went on down. We had three more to go and then another illuminated board slid by overhead; 500-550.

We turned back at right angles, traversing the same distance but three aisles farther along. There were several children and a couple of adults in the middle distance, getting stuff out of lockers. A tall, thin woman was a few yards away, trying to open a locker and put baggage in. Any other time I'd have helped her but tonight wasn't the night. There were two men in mid-distance, their luggage spread out round their feet.

My throat was dry as we went down the last few yards. The light shone blandly off the surface of the big metal locker. The plate over the lock with the legend 509 winked back at me. I swallowed once or twice. I looked at the girl. Her expression was one of almost complete indifference.

I knew then that whatever was troubling her conscience it wasn't the knocking over of Marcel Roco's payroll. One learns to read such things. Greed wasn't part of her makeup; and she certainly wasn't the criminal type. So I let her out. But I was still responsible for her safety. And I didn't aim to be taken off guard tonight.

I got the girl to stand shielding the entrance to the locker. It was just a precaution in case anyone had field glasses on us. The supposition was absurd as there was no high vantage point from which anyone could have deployed them but it was the mood I was in this evening.

Tina Matthews did like I said. I got out the key. I felt I'd hit the jackpot then. The numbers on the key-tag were in the same style as those on the locker itself. I put the key in the lock. It made a faint grating noise that set my teeth on edge. The girl looked at me openly.

Only her eyes showed a little strain like she was still hoping the key wouldn't fit; that her sister wasn't involved in anything underhand.

She might be right too. I tried the thing but it wouldn't move. The girl looked at me steadily.

'I don't think you've pushed it completely home, Mike.'

She reminded me of Stella then. But I didn't tell her that, of course.

There was a sweet click and the key turned smoothly and easily. The locker door swung slowly open. I had to force myself to look in the shadowy interior. There was a fairly substantial leather suitcase with gold-coloured locks taking up most of the available space. I didn't need to see the initials M.C. on the lid to know I'd won the kewpie doll.

I hadn't got time to note the girl's expression. I slid the case halfway out. It was as heavy as hell. I tried the clasps; they were locked, like I figured. Someone else would have had the keys. The case would have to be cut open. And this was neither the time nor the place for it. I put the Smith-Wesson back in my shoulder holster.

I got the case out, put it down on the floor. The jerk on my arm confirmed my earlier estimate. Unless it was all cut newspaper there was half a million inside all right. I savoured the sensation for just three seconds more. I put the locker-key back in the closed position and left it in situ.

I was just turning away when there was a shadow on the floor. It was the thin, blonde woman with the worn face who was having trouble with the locker opposite. She gave me a faded smile.

'Excuse me, sir. I wonder if you could help. I can't seem to turn the key.'

'Sure,' I said.

I stopped in mid-stride then, the muzzle of the big cannon half hidden in her handbag centred on my gut. She would have blown me halfway to San Francisco if she'd let it off. She smiled tightly at my expression and then swivelled the muzzle, aiming past me.

'Just take your hand off the Smith-Wesson, Mr Faraday. If you don't value your own life I'll kill the girl. You can take your choice.'

I looked at her eyes, did like she said. I put my hands where she could see them and folded them across my chest.

'That's better.'

She ignored Tina Matthews' frozen face, slightly altered her position to take in the two big men in dark suits who eased round the angle from the next aisle.

I knew who they'd be before they swam into focus. One was white-hair, the other the big wheelman who'd driven us out to Roco's place.

CHAPTER EIGHTEEN

1

White-hair's face was absolutely expression-less. He looked from me to the girl.

'Get his piece,' he said to the wheelman in the same soft casual voice.

The big man went in rear of the blonde woman and deftly removed the Smith-Wesson. I noticed he was limping. He picked up the case, grunting at the weight and went to stand next to white-hair.

The latter's lips hardly moved when he spoke.

'All right, Norah. You can beat it now. And thanks. Collect your cut at the usual place.'

The blonde woman nodded, closing her hand-bag with a snap. She ignored both me and the girl. She melted back round the end of the lockers, leaving the pile of luggage where it was. I turned to the girl but the white-haired man stopped me with a quick gesture.

'I'm not in the habit of exaggerating, Mr Faraday, as I'm sure you know. People don't get two chances in this business.'

'I take your meaning,' I said.

The corners of his mouth relaxed slightly.

'I thought you would. I gave you credit for being sensible. And innocent people would only get hurt in here. Shall we go?'

'Can we deal?' I said.

He shook his head.

'No deals.'

I stared from him to Tina Matthews' desperate face.

'Can we leave the girl out, then?'

He shook his head again. He tapped the suitcase at his feet with one polished shoe.

'We got to check all this stuff. And we can hardly do it here. Besides, Mr Roco wants to talk to the girl. He's curious about her part in all this.'

'She had no part,' I said.

White-hair shrugged.

'Then she can tell Mr Roco herself,' he said softly. 'Let's move. It's getting late and I have to be back here by morning.'

We moved like he said. The wheelman started to pick up the case but white-hair stopped him.

'We let Mr Faraday do that. Poetic justice.'

I picked up the case, the big man falling in behind me. The girl walked abreast of me as we went down the aisle. White-hair was slightly ahead but I knew better than to try anything. The man behind could drop both me and the girl before ever I swung the case.

'Back to the bungalow again?' I said. White-hair shook his head.

'Much more convenient this time. Though just as private. Mr Roco likes to move around.'

'I'll bet,' I said.

White-hair looked at me sharply.

'You look a little sick, Mr Faraday.'

'It's the airport,' I said. 'They always get me like this. I'm still suffering from jet-lag.'

The big wheelman was abreast of me now. The corners of his mouth eased back about two millimetres. These boys were certainly short on the humorous side. That's why I was working hard with the patter. We got outside the airport buildings and walked across between the masses of parked vehicles, the floodlights striking back glints from fenders and windshields.

'How did you get on to me?' I said.

White-hair shrugged.

'It wasn't a question of getting on to you, Mr Faraday. We had a call out. There were a lot of people involved.'

'It's the newest technology,' the wheelman said. 'Two-way radio and everything.'

'With all that working for you it's funny you didn't pick up the girl before she lit out with the money,' I said.

White-hair relaxed his lips slightly.

'I don't know anything about that,' he said softly. 'Mr Roco must have entrusted it to an amateur.'

'That lets Green in,' I said.

White-hair pursed his lips this time.

'Mr Green has been sweating some,' he said politely.

'My heap or yours?' I said.

We were up near the section where I'd parked the Buick.

'Both,' the wheelman said. 'The girl comes with me.'

He took hold of her by the arm. White-hair gave me a gentle glance.

'Mr Faraday and the money will be travelling with me. I'm sure there'll be no problems. Mr Faraday thinks too much of the young lady for that.'

I gave the girl what I hoped was a reassuring look.

'You're damn right,' I said.

The girl put her hand up alongside my face gently and then went off across the parking lot with the big man. I stared into white-hair's eyes.

'I wouldn't want anything to happen to her,' I told him.

He shrugged.

'That's entirely up to you. Nothing will so long as you behave.'

'I'll behave,' I said.

I walked with the suitcase over to the Buick, the lights throwing heavy shadows on the ground. I stashed the case on the rear seat, got behind the driving wheel. White-hair watched me, saying nothing. He waited until I started the engine before he got in the passenger seat.

'I'll tell you where,' he said pleasantly.

I pulled the Buick out and started off across

155

the lot. I hadn't gone a hundred yards before large, anonymous-looking black sedans fell in front and rear.

2

We drove for about half an hour to an unfamiliar section of town. We couldn't have been far from the coast as I could see moonlight shining on water as we breasted the rises leading into the foothills. White-hair signalled me off the secondary road up the winding drive of a large villa set back from the lane. There was a porch-light burning but the windows were masked with drapes because there wasn't any other light showing.

I guessed maybe the porch-light was some sort of signal. The first sedan had already stopped in front of the steps. I could see Tina Matthews going up with the big wheelman behind her. In rear of us as I drew the Buick in, came the crunching of gravel as the second sedan drew to a halt.

I got out the Buick and reached for the suitcase. White-hair stood and watched me. I went on up the steps toward the porch where the girl and the big man were waiting for us. There was a muffled conversation from behind. Then I heard the second sedan reversing back down the drive. I turned to see its lights flickering on the flowering hedges

156

before it drove off back toward L.A.

The case was heavier than I figured and I stopped for a moment on a sort of landing on the stone steps that zig-zagged up toward the porch. White-hair stood watching me from a couple of yards away. I gave myself a twisted smile in the semi-darkness.

I'd been calculating the odds. With the sedan gone I thought we might have more than an even chance. But it made no difference at all. There were still three men down at the foot of the steps. That left white-hair, the wheelman, Roco and maybe some others inside the house. There was no way out at all. And with the girl on my hands I was completely ham-strung.

I'd broken out once. They wouldn't let that happen again. White-hair looked at me like he could read my thoughts. He slowly inclined his head. I picked up the case and walked the last two yards to the porch. We were on a wide terrace now and I could see the ocean in the far distance, brilliantly lit by the clear, high moon.

The three men down by the sedan had a pack of cards out. They had them spread on the bonnet of the sedan and were playing a game like they were taking part in some musical comedy. We might have been on another planet. Except I knew they would be up here in three seconds flat in case of trouble.

The girl drew close to me as I put the case

down. Her fair hair shone in the light of the porch lamp. Her lips framed a two-word sentence.

'I'm frightened.'

I gave her a smile. It seemed to drop right off my face almost immediately but it was a smile nevertheless.

'It's all right,' I said. 'No harm will come to you.'

The girl shook her head slowly.

'I wasn't thinking about that, Mike.'

She came forward into my arms and I held her close to me for a moment. The big wheelman came up, his face impassive. He took the girl gently by the arm and slowly pulled her away. White-hair looked at me approvingly. The wheelman was opening the front door now. The hall gaped blackly beyond. He and the girl disappeared into the interior.

White-hair raised his eyebrows. I took the hint. I lifted the case and went on in front of him over the paved terrace to the big front door. The interior of the hall was warm and had a faint, elusive perfume. I couldn't see the others but I could sense their presence there in the darkness.

The front door closed behind us and I could hear white-hair buttoning off the porch light. Another light came on in the hallway itself as the wheelman got to a switch by the far door. I could see white walls; some paintings; and a few pieces of good furniture. But I wasn't here for the decor.

The girl had been wearing a lightweight white raincoat earlier this evening as though she felt cold and now she turned down the collar. There wasn't a sound from the rest of the house though I knew there were people here.

'Look after them,' white-hair said.

The big man moved over and stood between us and the front door. Not that I'd have tried anything. I knew he was armed but he looked so big and durable it would have needed a Sherman tank to stop him. The girl sat down on a leather chair that was set against the wall as white-hair went down the end of the corridor and opened the facing door. A bright shaft of light came out.

Then he went on in and the door closed softly behind him. I fumbled around in my pocket and came up with my package of cigarettes. I offered the pack to the big man. He grunted and took one. I lit it for him, smiling inwardly at the wary look in his eyes. Then I moved away and lit my own, feathering out blue smoke at the ceiling. I went to sit down on the case in the middle of the room.

We were still sitting there, like something out of a scene from Kafka, when the white-haired man came back.

CHAPTER NINETEEN

1

The girl and I walked into the big room with white-hair and the wheelman behind us. The latter took my Smith-Wesson out his pocket and put it down on a small ornamental table next to where he was standing by the door. It was too far away so I lost interest in it for the moment.

The place was got up as a study and business office. Incongruously, there was a big row of steel filing cabinets off at the left with a cleared floor space where we were standing. Then the Oriental carpet and the luxury began. There were two men in the room standing near the fireplace. I put the case down at my feet. The two men came over. One of them was Roco, like I'd expected. The other was Green, whom I hadn't expected.

The club manager marched straight over to me and hit me across the mouth. I rocked back on my heels and put my left into his gut. He doubled up in pain. White-hair smiled then, for the first and last time in the short period I'd known him.

'That will do,' Roco said.

He looked from me to the girl.

'Well, well,' he said. 'So you came back at

last.'

I glanced at Tina Matthews quickly. There was something here I didn't get. Green went back toward the fireplace, retching. Everyone else in the room ignored him. Roco took his gaze off the girl and transferred it to the case.

'I hope for your sake this contains the right merchandise,' he said.

'Would it make any difference if it didn't?' I said.

He slowly shook his head.

'Not for you,' he said softly. 'Bring it over here.'

The wheelman dragged the occasional table over from the door, holding the Smith-Wesson in his right. I put the case down on top of it. The girl was still standing near the filing cabinets. I was making a mental note of all this. One never knew. It might come in handy if we got lucky.

Green was back again, perspiration coating his face. He swallowed once or twice, avoiding my eyes.

'I told you it would come out all right, Mr Roco,' he said in a shaking voice.

'It was thanks to your dumbness we lost it in the first place,' Roco told him. 'All you have to do is keep quiet.'

Green bit back words that were coming to his lips. Instead he reached for his handkerchief and mopped his face. The others gathered round the table as Roco got out a

161

bunch of keys from his trousers pocket. I noticed that white-hair was standing well back. He didn't move a muscle but there was a deadliness in his repose that was far more impressive than the bluster of people like Green.

With personalities like him and Roco there was no need for flourishing pistols to impress the opposition.

I shifted my gaze from white-hair's face of hammered bronze to Green's. His features were paler even than usual beneath the black curly hair. Roco lifted the small key on its metal ring as though he were about to pronounce a benediction. The lighting in here shimmered on his short blond hair and he gave his strong yellow teeth a brief airing in an expression which evidently represented satisfaction.

He wore a dark brown suit on this occasion but he still retained the morocco leather shoes. You ought to be writing fashion notes for Harpers, Mike, I told myself. There was a suffocating silence in the study as Roco put the key in the first of the locks on the case. The click as he turned it seemed to tear a hole in the atmosphere.

Green coughed nervously, still holding the handkerchief to his face. Apart from the girl, standing back near the cabinets, momentarily forgotten by almost everyone; and white-hair between us and the door, everyone in the room, including myself, was concentrating on the case.

The blond-haired man selected a second key from the ring in his hand and put it in the left-hand lock. The resulting dick was followed by a hushed pause. Roco looked round quickly, then flung the lid back. If I was expecting cut newspapers then I was disappointed. Erika hadn't been smart enough for that.

Roco, Green, the wheelman and white-hair stood staring at the crisp bundles of bills that filled the case to overflowing. It was quite a moment. Roco stepped forward and riffled them with his forefinger, probing the piles to the bottom of the case. His lips moved silently.

I figured he was praying to himself but then I realised he was calculating the total amount by multiplying the stacks of notes. Green moved up, his face still streaked with perspiration.

'Is it all there?'

Roco shook his head with restrained fury. 'No thanks to you,' he said crisply.

He made an almost imperceptible movement of his eyebrows. The wheelman fired my Smith-Wesson at point-blank range. Green had an incredulous look on his face as he somersaulted across the room. There was a lot of blood on the front of his jacket. He hit a glassed-in bookcase and slid down in a tangle of broken fragments.

The girl had gasped and made a step forward but I signalled with my hand to stay back. No-one else moved. Roco shut the case and started re-locking it like he'd just swatted a fly. He looked at the wheelman approvingly.

'Green was coming apart at the seams,' he grunted.

He stared at me from under long-lashed eyelids.

'Too bad, Faraday. It's your gun, isn't it?'

I didn't say anything. I was still looking for a way out. White-hair moved then. He came farther into the room and whispered something to the wheelman. The big man, still carrying the Smith-Wesson, went back toward the door. He stood a yard or two away, his back to it, blocking the exit.

'Now we get back to you, Faraday,' Roco said. He smiled thinly at the girl.

'And I may have a few questions for you.'

'Can't we leave the girl out of it?' I said.

He shook his head.

'She's right in it. Same as you.'

His face had a curious expression. Presently I construed it as one of amusement.

'What story did she tell you? It seems to me you had the wrong end.'

I didn't know what the hell he was talking about but I plugged on anyway.

'Tina? She was merely worried about her sister.'

Roco's lip curled. He looked at the other

two men. I could see Green now. He moved slightly and then lay still. No-one else seemed to notice. That could be important. Or not. It was that sort of situation.

White-hair's hammered bronze face was impassive like usual. The wheelman licked his lips and shifted heavily on the balls of his feet. Roco's strange blue eyes were blazing. They looked more like those of a doll than ever. It was a weird contrast to the calmness of his face. He lifted the case and put it down at the side of the table.

'You're so dumb, Faraday, it hardly seems possible. This isn't Tina! It's her sister, Erika!'

We were still standing like some frozen sort of tableau when heavy feet sounded in the hall, the door burst inward and something that looked like a hand grenade bounced into the centre of the room.

2

The wheelman seemed like he was paralysed. He had the Smith-Wesson half-raised as I went across the study in a long dive, catching the girl around the knees. We went down behind the row of heavy metal filing cabinets as a great, eye-searing brilliance filled the whole room.

I never heard any explosion, merely watched the ceiling coming in in a boiling cloud of slow-motion dust. I dragged the girl over against the cabinets, felt them quiver with the viciousness of the blast. There were screams now and fragments of metal whining about the room.

The wheelman was sagging, going toward the floor, blood running from what was left of his mouth. I saw white-hair in the same split-second. He was rolled into a bundle, making for the window. He went crashing through into the darkness outside. I saw blood on his coat sleeve but otherwise he seemed unharmed. He was a pro all right.

Most of the screaming was coming from Roco. His face was black, his blond hair scorched and streaked with blood. It came from hundreds of tiny punctures on the front of his suit. He was scrabbling aimlessly around in the smoke, looking for the suitcase.

That had been thrown up against the far wall by the blast, most of which had gone up into the ceiling. The handle of the case was lying quite close to Green. He'd escaped the glass too though the front of the bookcase was all shattered and broken. As I watched his hand came out as though by instinctive reflex and touched the case.

These characters are fond of money even when they're dying, Mike, I told myself. The thought helped me to get through a few bad moments. I could hear shots now, coming from the garden outside. It seemed like a good idea to stay behind the cabinets until I could see

166

what the score was.

Roco was still screaming, automatically now. He was trying to beat the flames on his clothing out. He went back into the smoke and I could hear breaking glass. The noise he was making seemed to go on for a long time. Presently the smoke cleared and I could see him again. His arms moved feebly and then he lay still.

The girl stirred beneath me then. I put my mouth close to her ear.

'You all right?'

'Yes, Mike, I think so. Oughtn't we to get out?'

I shook my head.

'We don't know what the hell's going on. Best to stay put until we see what's happening. Whoever threw that grenade in was no friend of Roco's.'

The girl shuddered. I helped her up until she was sitting with her back against the cabinets. I found out later that they'd been shifted over two feet forward with the strength of the blast. I could see the room curtains smouldering now. It was a wonder the whole house wasn't on fire.

I heard an automobile gun up from the far distance. Then there was silence. I went to sit near the girl, watching her face. The glasses were on the floor somewhere near her and I crawled over and picked them up. I squinted through the lenses. They were plain glass. I grinned at the girl and lit a cigarette, feathering out the smoke gratefully.

'Tina or Erika? Which is it?'

There was something shimmering in the corners of the girl's eyes.

'I'm sorry, Mike. I didn't want to deceive you. But my life was in danger too. I wanted to tell you about it at dinner. But the moment passed.'

'You'd better tell me about it now,' I said. 'Before the law arrives. We may need to synchronise our stories. Don't forget Green has a slug from my Smith-Wesson in him.'

The Matthews girl nodded. While she was collecting her thoughts I went over to the wheelman. There wasn't much left of his face and there was nothing I could do for him. Green and Roco could wait. I found the Smith-Wesson still clutched in the wheelman's stiffening fingers, retrieved it.

I crawled back to the girl. She looked at me somewhat defiantly, the colour coming into her face.

'Sure, I went out with Roco a few times a while back, Mike,' she said defensively. 'I didn't know what he was like. When I found out I wouldn't have anything more to do with him. He'd found someone else by then.'

I tipped some ash off the end of my cigarette on to what was left of the floor.

'Your sister Tina,' I said.

Erika nodded, her eyes fixed in front of her

like the smoke and the shattered remains of the room didn't exist. There was still some faint firing coming from the garden. I got up, found what was left of the drinks cabinet, squirted the contents of a soda syphon over the blazing curtains until the flames went out.

'Tina was young and impressionable,' Erika Matthews said. 'She'd never had a taste of the bright lights before. She was a librarian. Nothing I said did any good. I just had to sit and watch her being destroyed.'

'Tough,' I said.

'It was, Mike. I didn't intend to deceive you. Honestly. I was frightened for my own life.'

'Did you know Tina had taken that money?' I said.

Erika shook her head.

'Not directly. I knew something bad was going on. When she gave me the package that night I guessed maybe she was going away. But I thought with Roco. Not that money was involved.'

'So you didn't know where she'd gone?' I said.

The girl looked at me with sombre eyes.

'No. She didn't say where. I guess she's dead, isn't she?'

'That's something I can't figure,' I said. 'She lit out with the payroll and stashed it at L.A. International. Then she flew out somewhere herself. Green was supposed to keep an eye on her for Roco. The pay-off was at The Blue

Parrot. But he bungled it and she lit out.'

I looked at her through a wreath of tobacco smoke.

'You figured if you could use me, masquerading as Tina, something might break loose in Roco's organisation. You told the club you were going up to Lake Arrowhead and then changed your personality to that of Tina.'

The girl smiled faintly.

'It wasn't too hard, Mike. We were twins. No-one outside the family could ever tell us apart. I left the apartment. I knew Roco and I was frightened when Tina went missing. I only went back there because I'd given you that address. I'd taken some things over to a girl-friend's and lay low there.'

I stared at Erika for a long moment.

'So Roco was looking at Lake Arrowhead. He must have guessed what had happened and that you were in on it.'

I remembered then Green's puzzlement when I'd mentioned Tina. Remembered too the girl taking the card off her sister's gift. Because it would have said; From Tina to Erika.

'Roco knew Tina had been taken out, perhaps by Green, before the stolen money turned up. That was why he was so burned. But when he heard I'd been retained by Tina that brought him out the woodwork.'

I took the cigarette from my mouth and stared at the girl.

170

'As no doubt you intended,' I said.

The girl shook her head. Her eyes were pleading now.

'I was using you, Mike. Yes. But not deceiving you.'

'It doesn't matter now,' I said.

We were still sitting there when the room was suddenly filled with blue uniforms. I got up. 'About time,' I said.

I helped Erika to her feet, steadied her as we looked around the shambles of the room. One of the men went over to Roco, turned him on his back.

'He's gone all right,' he reported to a tall man in the uniform of a Captain. I stared incredulously as the officer's face resolved into that of the under-manager of the Sheraton-Plaza.

'Aren't you pleased to see me, Mr Faraday?' he said.

He grinned.

'I had to choose between you and the suitcase. It was a piece of tricky bowling there! But I figured the cabinets would shield you and the girl.'

I was still trying to figure this out when the door opened and Harry Popkiss came in.

CHAPTER TWENTY

1

Popkiss nodded at me familiarly, like he'd just come in for a quiet game of bridge and went over to the sprawled figure of Green in the corner.

'He'll live,' he grunted.

He gave me a humorous look.

'You might even pin all this on him.'

'Some hopes,' I said. 'Since when were you Chief of Police?'

He grinned again.

'Since tonight. Since before your secretary rang. We had some costumes left over from a fancy dress ball at the hotel last year. I decided to use them.'

'And a few grenades left over from the Vietnam War,' I said.

He made an admonitory clicking noise with his tongue.

'That was a little embellishment we thought up on the spur of the moment. I happen to know a large-scale arms dealer who supplies a lot of countries in the Middle East. He broke open his stores at short notice.'

I stared round the room, biting back my rising anger.

'Sure,' I said. 'And you might have gotten us

both killed.'

Popkiss shook his head.

'You were already in danger, remember? We just saved your lives. Or to be more specific Leo did. You don't think Roco would have left you alive, do you? But don't bother to thank us.'

I stared at him for a moment.

'I'm sorry,' I said. 'These sort of shoot-outs where I'm left as sitting duck in the middle tend to aggravate one's nerves.'

Popkiss chuckled. He dragged a couple of chairs over, sat the girl and myself down.

'You need a shot.'

The under-manager went across to the buffet in the corner and came back with a bottle of cognac and some glasses. He rinsed them out, poured the spirit on the floor and started again. Erika and I got the first shot down us. It tasted good.

'You took your time,' I said.

Popkiss shrugged.

'We had to get rid of the opposition outside first.'

I stared at the man in the uniform of a police captain.

'You have a pretty peculiar staff,' I said. He shook his head.

'We have a pretty good staff, Mr Faraday,' he said harshly. 'Not much they wouldn't do for me. And I pay accordingly. Which reminds me . . .' He bent to the suitcase, looked at its contents with satisfaction.

'It seems to be all here.'

'Plus your fifty per cent interest,' I said. He smiled.

'Business is business.'

He reached in his coat-pocket, came out with a big envelope which crackled. He threw it across to me. I caught it and held it, saying nothing.

'I hope that will sufficiently recompense you, Mr Faraday. You have done splendidly.'

'You haven't asked me what the hell it was all about yet,' I said.

He shrugged.

'You've only just found out yourself. But your secretary can put it all in your report, when you send me my receipt.'

I grinned, stubbing out my cigarette on the floor. I didn't want to start another fire with all this money lying around. It gives one a different attitude when some of it's your own.

'What else do I have to do for this?' I said.

Popkiss shrugged again, looking around the room. His massive bulk seemed to exude confidence. Despite the heat of the night he was wearing a belted raincoat which made him look more like someone out of a forties Warner movie than ever. Raincoats seemed to be popular this evening.

The girl had her eyes closed as she drained her glass.

'You didn't see a guy with white hair

outside,' I said.

'He got away,' Popkiss said crisply. 'He was one of the best pros around, I should say.'

He looked across at the burnt thing on the floor.

'Apart from Roco and this man by the door.'

'How am I going to explain all this?' I said. 'Green there has one of my slugs in him.'

'You'll think of something,' Popkiss said imperturbably. 'You always have in the past.'

He became brisk, handed the case over to one of the blue uniformed men.

'We have to move, Mr Faraday. Your secretary obviously will not have neglected to inform the police who must certainly be here soon.'

His eyes sparkled with humour.

'We would not want any confusion or misunderstanding about our little charade.'

'Money sure sweetens your temper,' I said.

Popkiss chuckled softly.

'I am not alone in that,' he said.

'How the hell did you pick us up at the airport?' I said. 'You must have followed us here. And I suppose Deborah had a hand in it, too.'

'She is waiting outside in the car as a matter of fact,' he said smugly.

He glanced briefly at Roco.

'He is not the only one with a large organisation. I can muster quite a few people. And we have the use of helicopters, two-way radio and other sophisticated gadgets. You haven't been out of my sight, metaphorically speaking, since you accepted my commission. But I appreciated the young lady's call, which I intercepted in my car on my way here. It told me you were on the level.'

'If you have such sophisticated gadgets,' I said, 'you might get a message through to Stella. She only worries otherwise. You know what women are.'

'I do indeed, Mr Faraday,' he said equably. 'But it has already been done. She knows that you are safe.'

'I appreciate it,' I said. 'And since you're being so magnanimous you'd better take this young lady with you.'

Popkiss gave me a wry look. He glanced around the wrecked room for the last time.

'I will see you when this is over, Mr Faraday. That envelope does not represent the full extent of my appreciation.'

'I should think not,' I said. 'I hear dinner at the Sheraton-Plaza is out of this world.'

Popkiss grinned, turning to follow the blue-uniformed men. The girl hesitated on her way to the door.

'I'd rather stay with you, Mike.'

I shook my head.

'It will be easier if I tell the story my own way. There's no need for them to know you're involved. Though your sister's part will have to come out. Popkiss was my client, not you. We

176

didn't find the money, of course.'

I gave a wry look at the sprawled figures of Green, Roco and the wheelman. Being a pro comes hard at times.

'White-hair was the heavy,' I said. 'The police will be looking for him.'

The girl stared at me anxiously.

'You figure they'll find him, Mike?'

I grinned again.

'What do you think.'

I sat and listened to the footsteps of all those people going away from the villa and poured myself another cognac. Then I went over to make Green more comfortable. He was groaning now. I poured some of the raw spirit down his throat. He gagged and his eyes opened.

I left him and went back to the chair, lit another cigarette. I was still sitting there, sipping cognac and smoking, feeling the bulk of the Smith-Wesson against my chest, thinking about nothing in particular, when the faint sound of sirens coming up the canyon started to split the silence.

2

'So you still keep your licence?' Stella said incredulously.

I looked at her critically.

'Of course,' I said. 'When did I ever lose it?'

177

Stella gave the elegant little noise that passes for a snort with her. Today it was raining and streams of moisture made a blurred surface of the windows and masked the automobiles on the boulevard. She came over from her desk and stood looking down at me, her arms folded over firm breasts.

She wore a smart two-piece number, the skirt of which was riding up over her knees in a way which was starting to make me fidget in my swivel chair. Stella's knees do things to me that full exposure of another woman in a nudie movie fails to stir. She's that sort of girl.

'McGiver bought it in the end,' I said. 'He had to. With Roco dead and a few other assorted plug-uglies, it's cleaned up a few scummy corners around L.A. that the police hadn't been able to reach.'

'Someone will soon take their places,' Stella said.

'Of course,' I said.

I stared at her closely.

'Since when did you become cynical?'

'As of now,' Stella said. 'Seeing you get away with murder.'

I spread my hands wide on the blotter.

'I didn't murder anyone on this case,' I said. 'I was the murderee and potential victim throughout.'

Stella smiled. I could have watched it all morning.

'How about coffee?' I said. 'I think I've

178

earned it.'

'You earned more than that,' Stella said happily.

I sat there salivating, listening to her switch on the percolator and clatter around with cups and saucers. She came back after a bit and sat on a corner of my desk.

'Why didn't Roco turn Tina's place over before?' she said. 'Especially since she'd been gone some time.'

'He had a reason,' I said. 'The other girl was living there for one. For another Green had blown things. He was ordered to get Tina. McGiver had that from Green himself.'

'He'll live, then?' Stella said.

I nodded.

'With time and care. They interviewed him just after surgery. He's giving them all he knows about Roco's organisation. That way he'll draw a lighter sentence.'

'You were telling me about Roco and the girl's apartment,' Stella reminded me. 'Why he didn't turn the place over.'

'He was keeping tabs,' I said. 'When he heard I was employed by Tina he figured she'd come back to pick up the money. Erika was keeping out of the way, of course. She was using me to flush Roco into the open. She arranged for a friend to send Leroy a pre-written card from Arrowhead. But Tina was already dead by then.'

'Dead?'

Stella looked at me with sombre eyes.

I nodded.

'That was why Roco ordered Green taken out. He fouled things up all along the line. Firstly, by leaving Roco's girl-friend alone with half a million dollars of laundered money around. He tracked her to L.A. International after she'd stashed the money and given her sister the locker key. He shot and wounded her. Somehow she got aboard her scheduled flight.'

I stared down into the littered contents of the earthenware ashtray on my desk.

'She must have had a fantastic constitution. Or maybe money or the prospect of it keeps people alive after they should be dead.'

Stella shivered suddenly. She went back to fetch the coffee, put my cup on the blotter. Then she crossed to sit in the client's chair, stirring her own cup in silence.

'How do you know all this, Mike?' she said softly.

'The police pieced it all together from Green. Tina got to San Francisco. She reported in at a hospital under a false name. She'd left all her stuff in a hotel so there was nothing to identify her. She died in the hospital a few days later of the gunshot wound. Erika flew up yesterday to identify the body.'

Stella's eyes were very clear and very blue as she stared at me.

'With her dream of half a million dollars

lying in an airport locker, Mike.'

I sat up straight in my chair, stirred my coffee. I felt like a thousand years old.

'It's a phoney dream,' I said. 'But one shared by millions of people all over the world.' Stella became more brisk.

'Still, Erika made out all right in the end.' I stared across at her.

'A three-year contract from Harry Popkiss to sing in cabaret at the Sheraton-Plaza can't be bad.'

'It isn't,' I said. 'Especially as we shall be joining them there for dinner tomorrow night.'

'You didn't tell me,' Stella said accusingly.

'I didn't want you wasting half your salary on a new dress,' I said.

Stella made a moue. She was trying hard not to laugh.

'The salary you pay me wouldn't buy me a half a pair of earrings.'

'I'll pretend I didn't hear that,' I said.

When Stella had finished laughing she came up with another question.

'There's only one snag about Green, Mike. Harry Popkiss' part, I mean.'

I shook my head.

'Green was out when Popkiss turned up. So he's in the clear. The last thing Green remembers is the wheelman shooting him.'

Stella frowned.

'So the white-haired man was never found.'

I stared down into the dark surface of my

coffee. 'He was a pro,' I said. 'Like me.'

'But it hardly seems fair, Mike,' Stella said. 'Popkiss creaming off half a million dollars like that.'

'We were wrong again,' I said. 'Popkiss just announced he's giving a quarter million dollars to charity.'

I grinned at her.

'It's good for his political image. And he gets tax relief on it.'

I leaned forward in my chair.

'Talking of money,' I said. 'There's an envelope over on your desk. Underneath the typewriter. It's a little spreading of Popkiss' largesse.'

Stella went over, came back with the envelope, opened it up. She stared at the cheque, little flushes starting on her cheeks.

'Mike, you shouldn't have . . .'

'I know,' I said. 'But like you said, you need a new outfit.'

Stella put her arms round my neck. When I came down from the ceiling she looked at me sidewise, patting a stray hair into place on her immaculate coiffeur.

'It's been a unique case for you, Mike.'

'Why?' I said.

She shook her head.

'No bodies along the way.'

I grinned.

'We made up for it at the end.'

I handed my empty cup to Stella. I was

beginning to feel muzzy again. The case had gone so fast I was still spinning. Stella came back and put the cup down.

'I like Erika a lot better without her spectacles,' I said.

I stared at her.

'You know they had nothing but plain glass in them?'

Stella stared at me too.

'You feel all right, Mike?'

'Still suffering from jet-lag,' I said.

We hope you have enjoyed this Large Print book. Other Chivers Press or Thorndike Press Large Print books are available at your library or directly from the publishers.

For more information about current and forthcoming titles, please call or write, without obligation, to:

Chivers Large Print
published by BBC Audiobooks Ltd
St James House, The Square
Lower Bristol Road
Bath BA2 3BH
UK
email: bbcaudiobooks@bbc.co.uk
www.bbcaudiobooks.co.uk

OR

Thorndike Press
295 Kennedy Memorial Drive
Waterville
Maine 04901
USA
www.gale.com/thorndike
www.gale.com/wheeler

All our Large Print titles are designed for easy reading, and all our books are made to last.